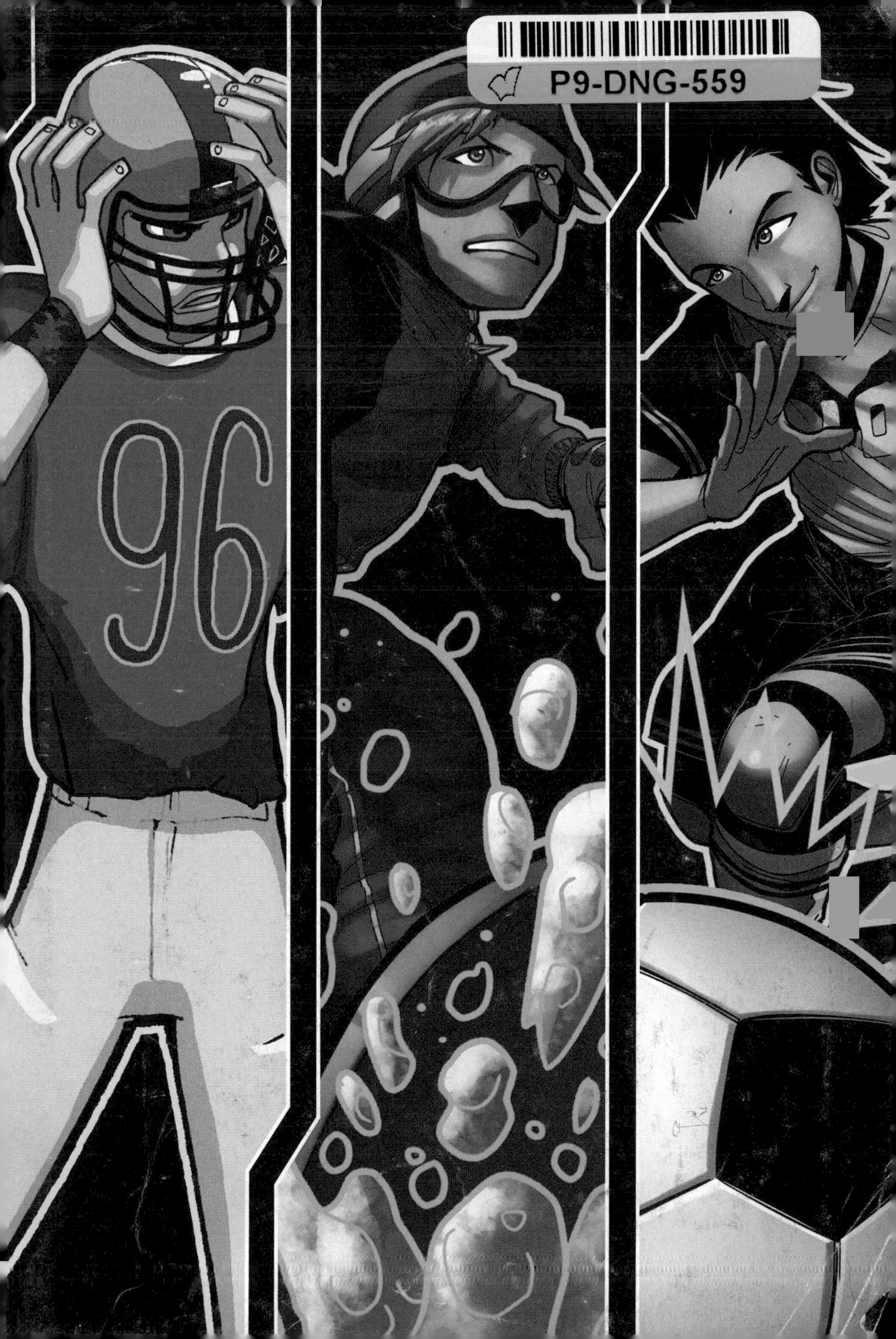
96

UP NEXT ›››

on Sports Illustrated KIDS

:02 SPORTS ZONE SPECIAL REPORT

:04 FEATURE PRESENTATION:

SACK ATTACK!

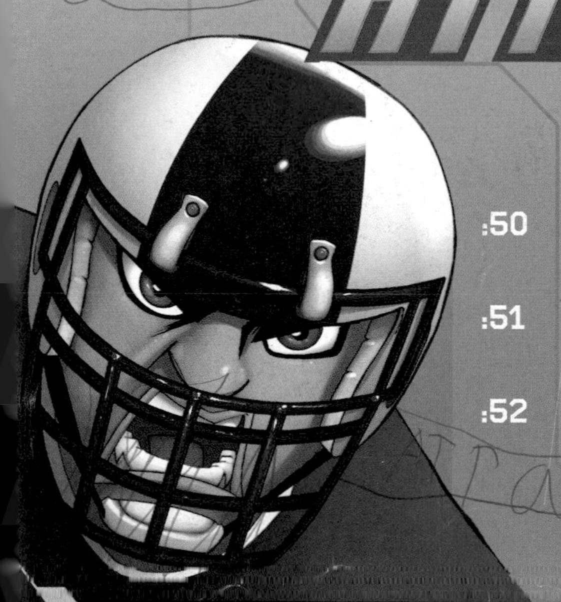

FOLLOWED BY:

:50 SPORTS ZONE POSTGAME RECAP

:51 SPORTS ZONE POSTGAME EXTRA

:52 SI KIDS INFO CENTER

OP DEFENSIVE LINEMAN MIKE BRAVIS PREPARES TO FACE JAR

SIK TICKER

SPORTS ZONE

SPECIAL REPORT

FBL
FOOTBALL

PNT
PAINTBALL

SOC
SOCCER

BSL
BASEBALL

BBL
BASKETBALL

HKY

UNSTOPPABLE FORCE TO MEET IMMOVABLE OBJECT

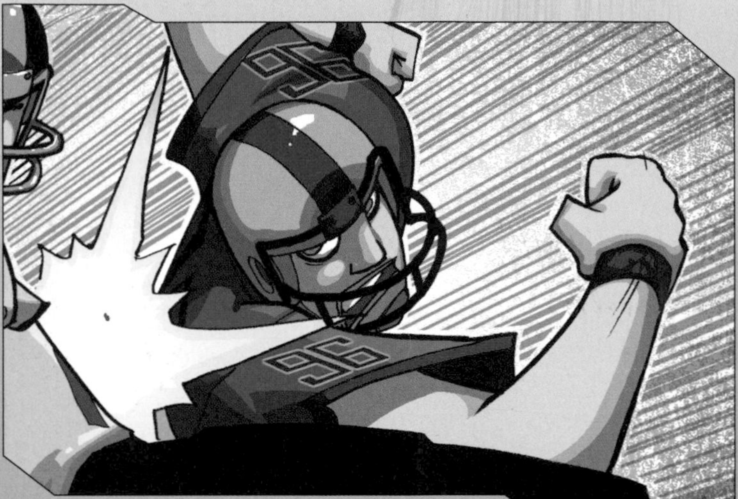

MIKE BRAVIS

STATS:
AGE: 14
POSITION: DEFENSIVE LINEMAN

BIO: As far as athleticism goes, Mike Bravis is almost unstoppable. He knows how to use his large frame to overpower offensive linemen, and his speed allows him to shut down outside runs with ease. But recently, Mike's been taking some heat for not preparing for his opponents. Powering through the opposition has worked so far, but Mike hasn't faced someone as big as Jared Michaels yet.

Sports Illustrated KIDS

UP NEXT: SACK ATTACK!

BLZ vs BKS
3-1
TGR vs RDR
33-32
EAG vs BAN
14-7
SPA vs WLD
4-3
BAN vs RDR
21-15
RZR vs LIG
4-3
BLZ vs BKS
3-1

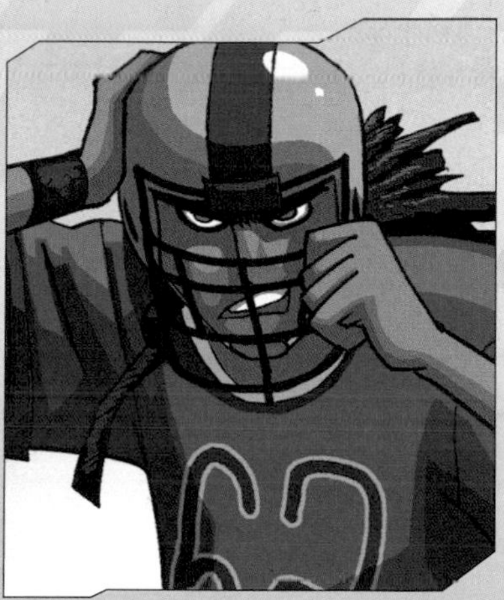

TRENTON KUBRICK

AGE: 14

POSITION: DEFENSIVE LINEMAN

BIO: Most people think Trenton is a gifted defensive player, but Trenton sees himself as a hard worker with very little natural ability. He believes that preparation and technique will beat pure talent every time.

JARED MICHAELS

AGE: 15

BIO: Jared is one of the biggest and strongest offensive linemen in the state. He hasn't given up a single sack all year.

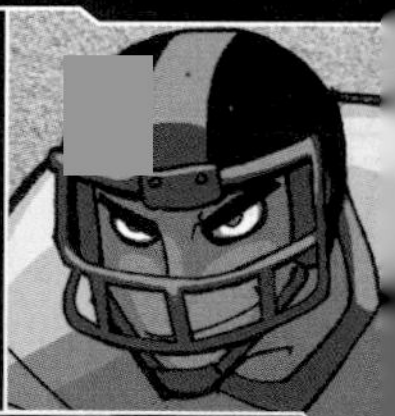

COACH GAVIN

AGE: 37

BIO: Coach Gavin teaches his players to play to their strengths while also working on their weaknesses.

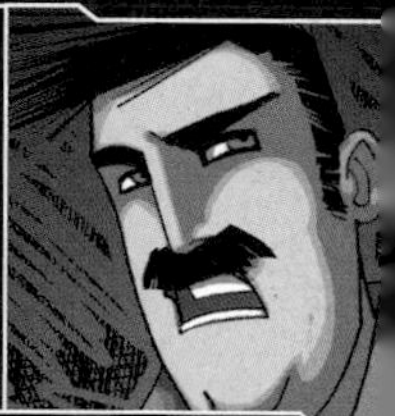

CARTER COOLEY

AGE: 14

BIO: Easygoing and friendly, Carter gets along with nearly all of his teammates.

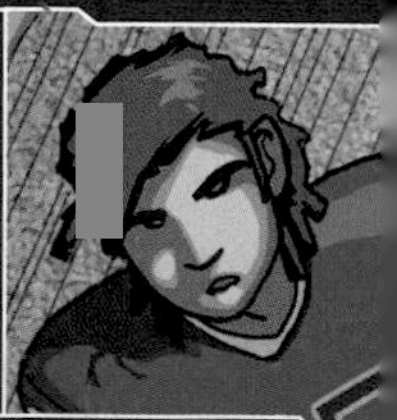

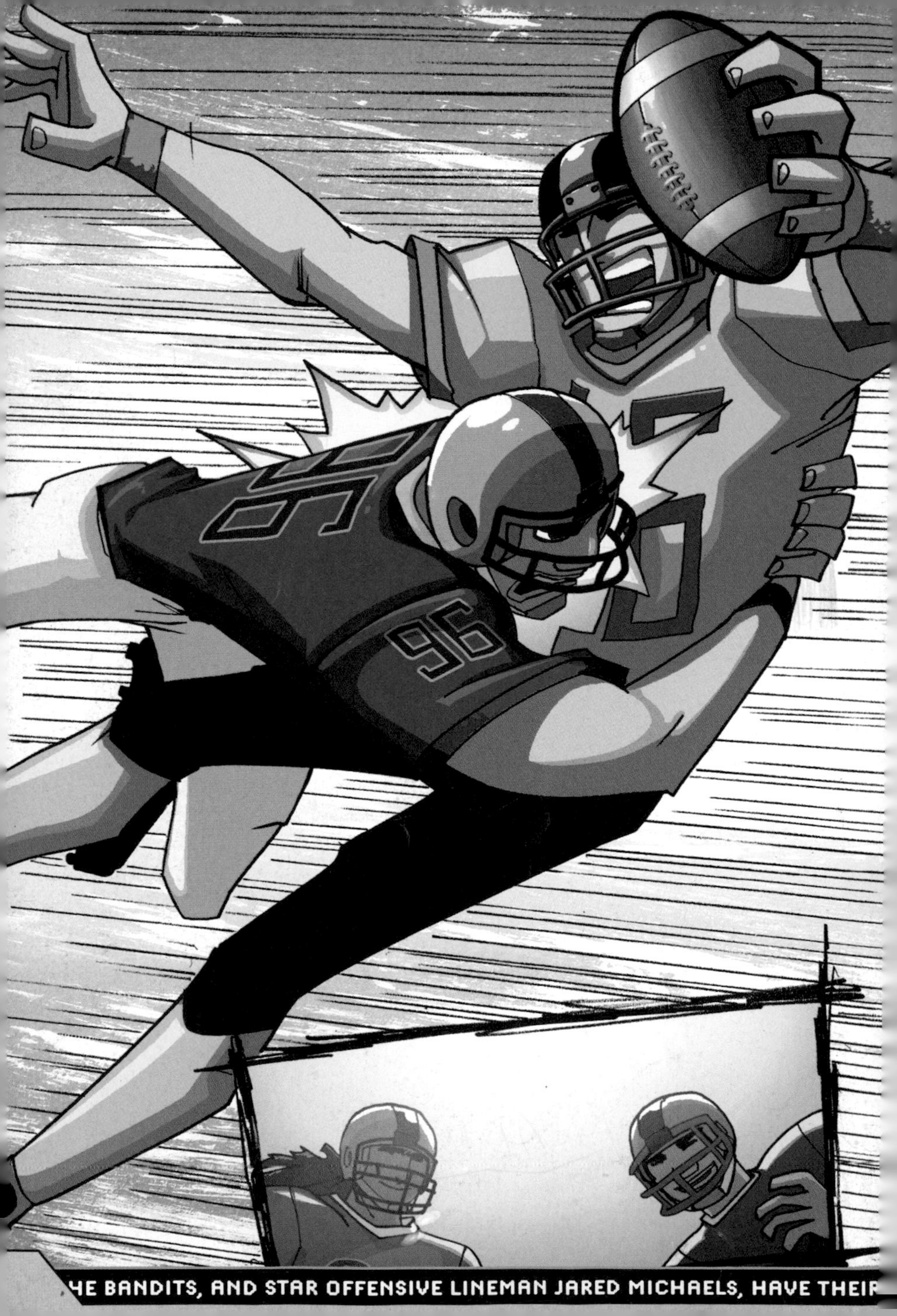
HE BANDITS, AND STAR OFFENSIVE LINEMAN JARED MICHAELS, HAVE THEIR

Sports Illustrated KIDS

PRESENTS

SACK ATTACK!

A PRODUCTION OF

STONE ARCH BOOKS
a capstone imprint

written by Blake A. Hoena
illustrated by Gerardo Sandoval
colored by Benny Fuentes

designed and directed by Bob Lentz
edited by Sean Tulien
editorial management by Donald Lemke
creative direction by Heather Kindseth
editorial direction by Michael Dahl

Sports Illustrated KIDS *Sack Attack!* is published by Stone Arch Books,
151 Good Counsel Drive, P.O. Box 669, Mankato, Minnesota 56002.
www.capstonepub.com

Printed in the United States of America in Stevens Point, Wisconsin.
032011 006111WZF11

Summary: The Eagles have two talented defensive linemen: Mike Bravis outmuscles his opponents, while Trenton Kubrick prefers to outsmart them. The two defensive stars may have different playstyles, but the outcome is always the same: they get the sacks while their opponents get embarrassed. But the best offensive lineman in the league is coming to town, so Trenton and Mike will have to combine their talents to stop him.

Library of Congress Cataloging-in-Publication Data
Hoena, B. A.
Sack attack! / written by Blake A. Hoena ; illustrated by Gerardo Sandoval and Benny Fuentes.
p. cm. -- (Sports illustrated kids graphic novels)
ISBN-13: 978-1-4342-2243-5 (library binding)
ISBN-13: 978-1-4342-3404-9 (pbk.)
1. Football--Comic books, strips, etc. 2. Football stories. 3. Graphic novels. [1. Graphic novels. 2. Football--Fiction.] I. Sandoval, Gerardo, ill. II. Fuentes, Benny, ill. III. Title. IV. Series: Sports illustrated kids graphic novels.
PZ7.7.H64Sac 2012
741.5973--dc22 2011006766

S SET ON TAKING DOWN THE HIGH-FLYING, PLAYOFF-BOUND EAGLE SIK TICKER

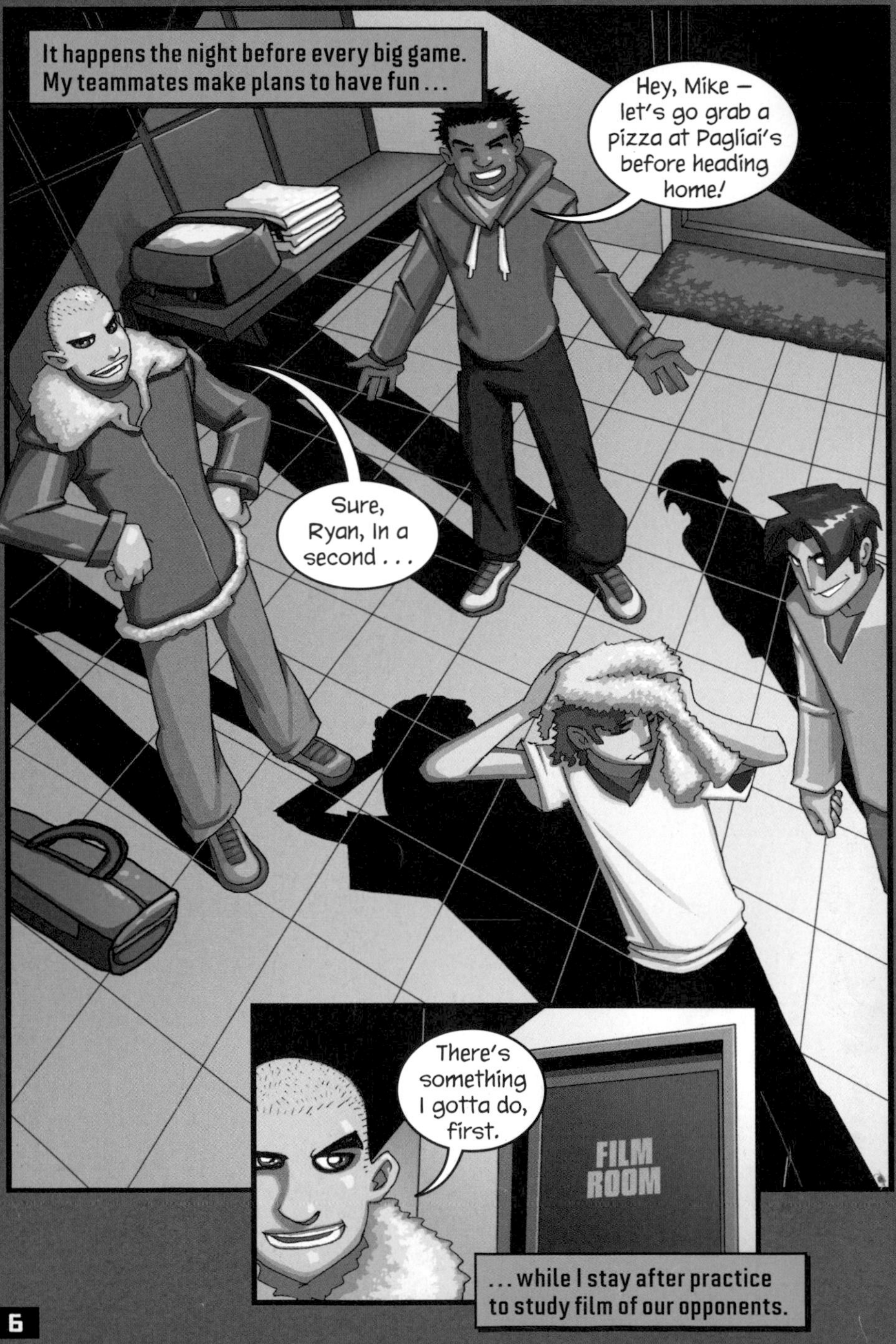
It happens the night before every big game. My teammates make plans to have fun . . .
Hey, Mike — let's go grab a pizza at Pagliai's before heading home!
Sure, Ryan, in a second . . .
There's something I gotta do, first.
FILM ROOM
. . . while I stay after practice to study film of our opponents.

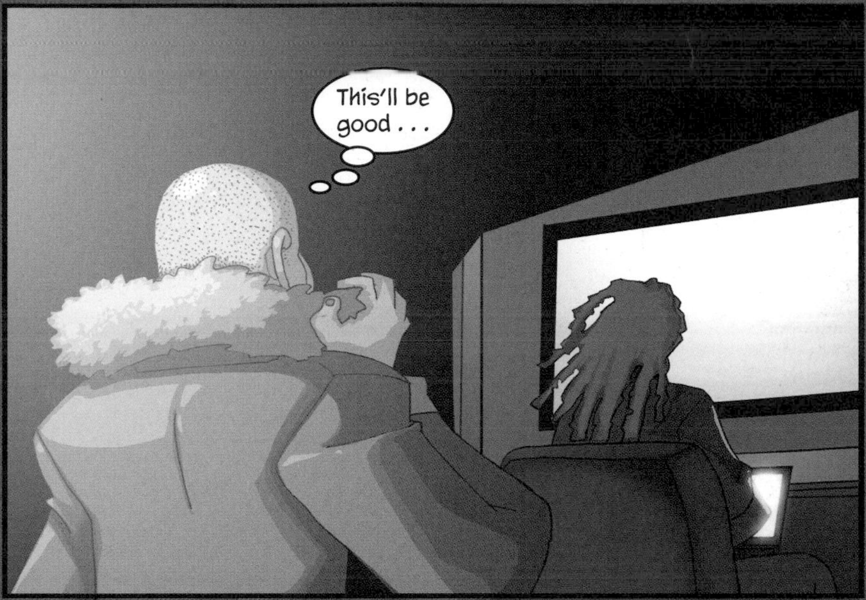
This'll be good . . .

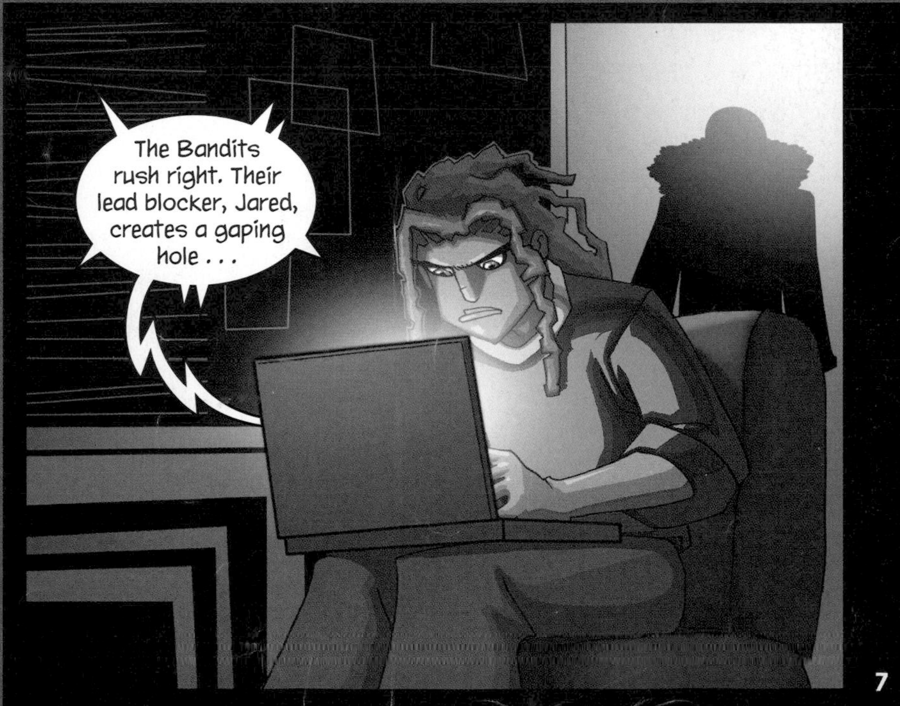
The Bandits rush right. Their lead blocker, Jared, creates a gaping hole . . .

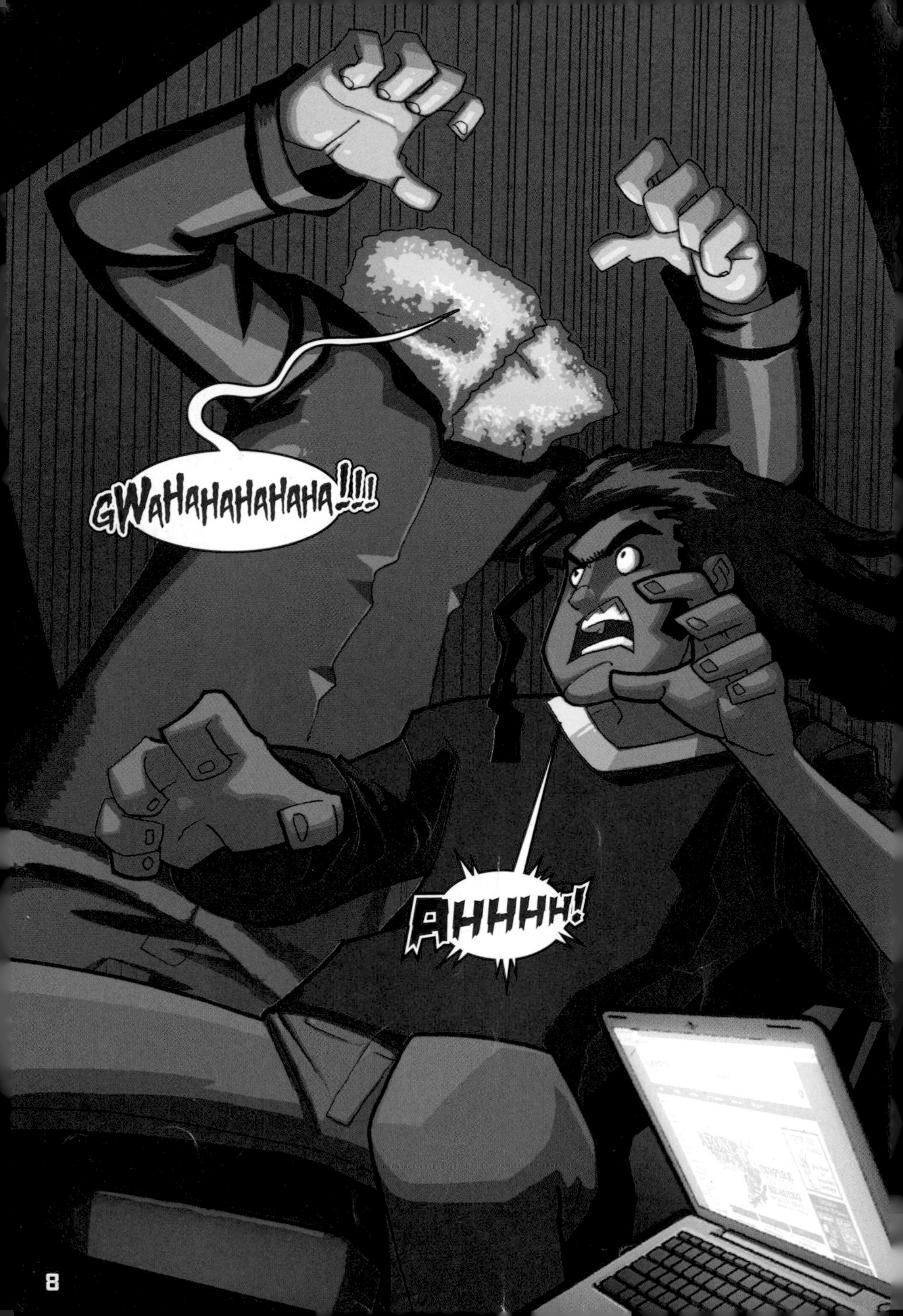
GWAHAHAHAHAHA!!!!
AHHHH!

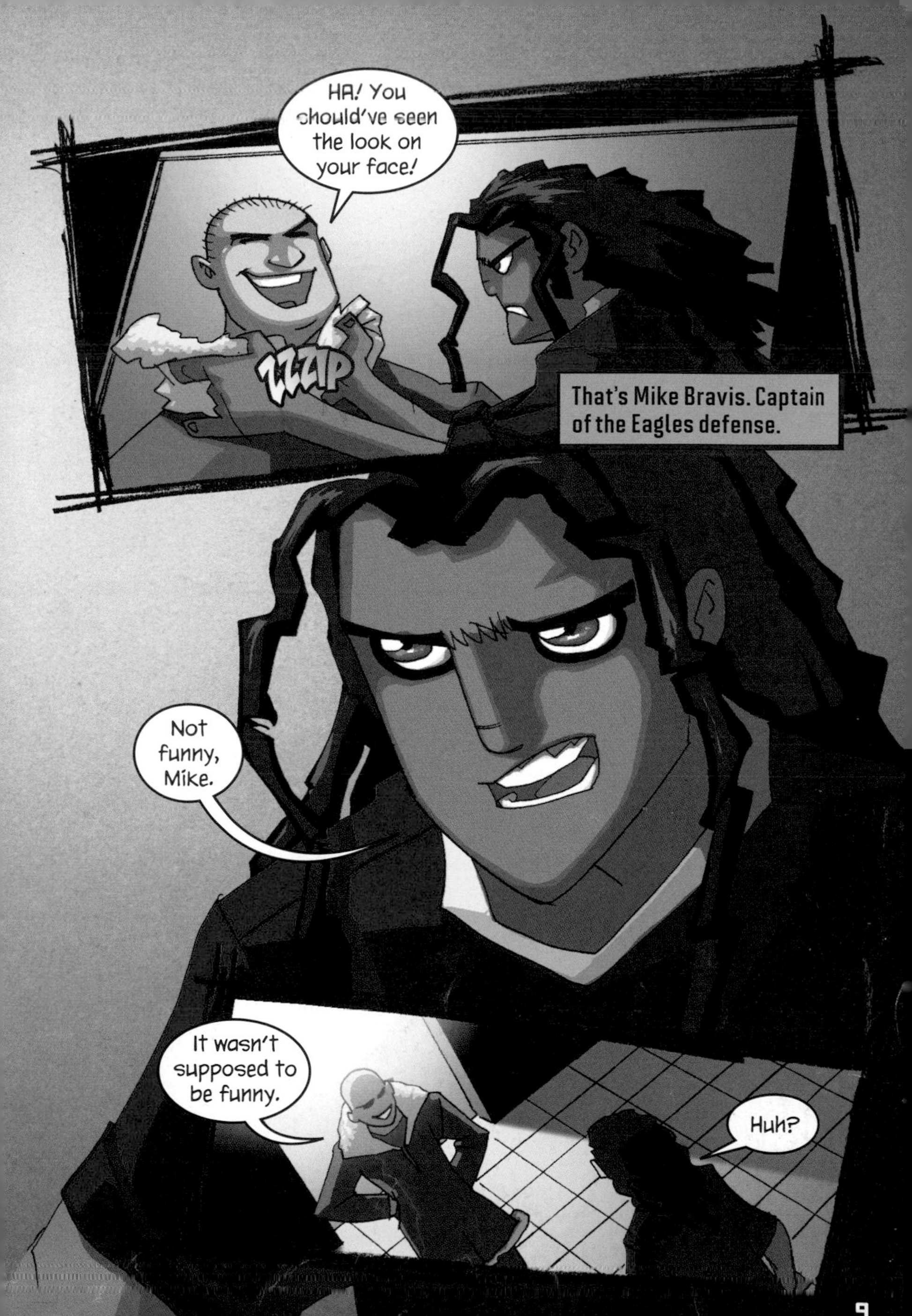

HA! You should've seen the look on your face!
ZZZIP
That's Mike Bravis. Captain of the Eagles defense.
Not funny, Mike.
It wasn't supposed to be funny.
Huh?

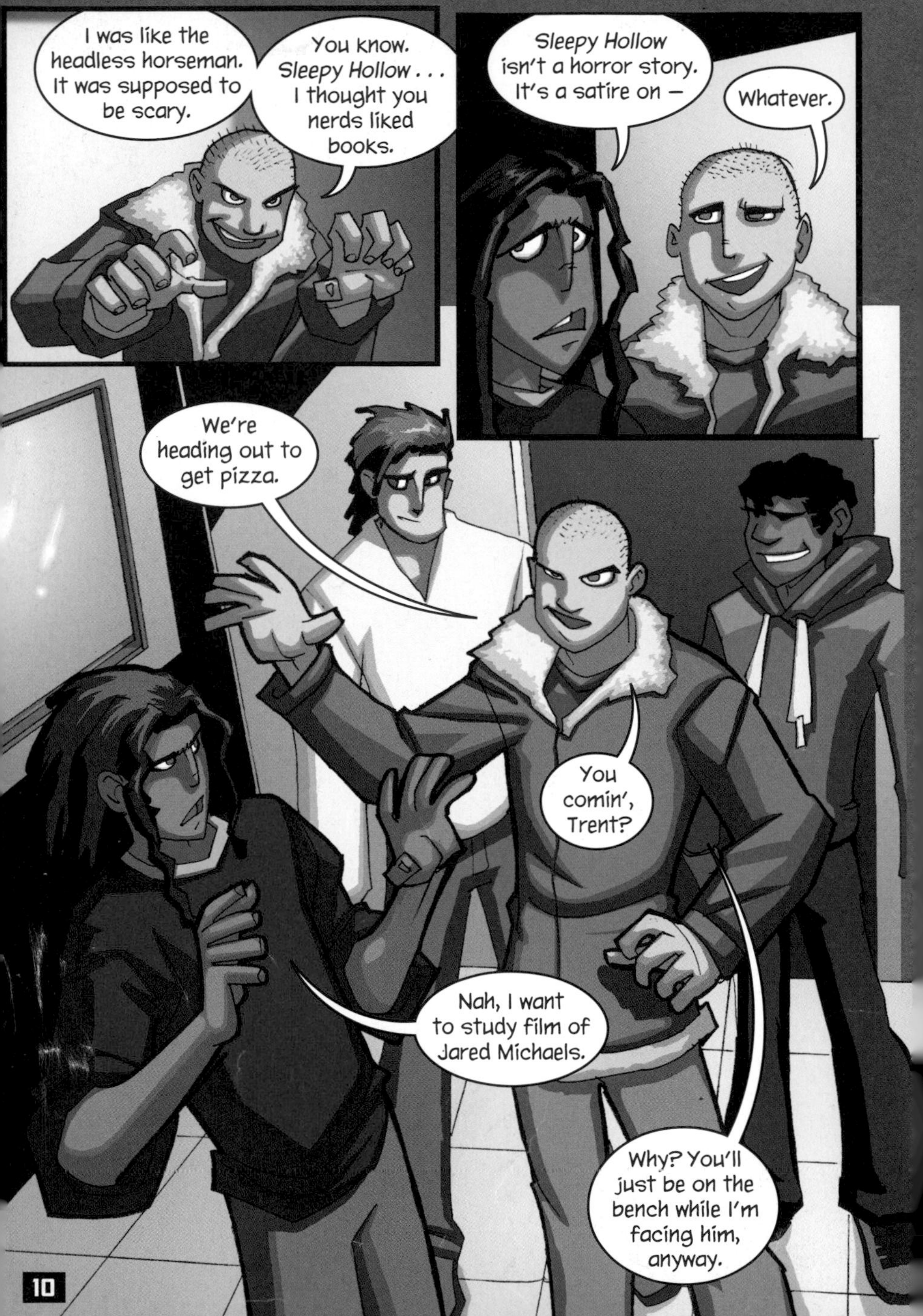
I was like the headless horseman. It was supposed to be scary.
You know. *Sleepy Hollow* . . . I thought you nerds liked books.
Sleepy Hollow isn't a horror story. It's a satire on –
Whatever.
We're heading out to get pizza.
You comin', Trent?
Nah, I want to study film of Jared Michaels.
Why? You'll just be on the bench while I'm facing him, anyway.

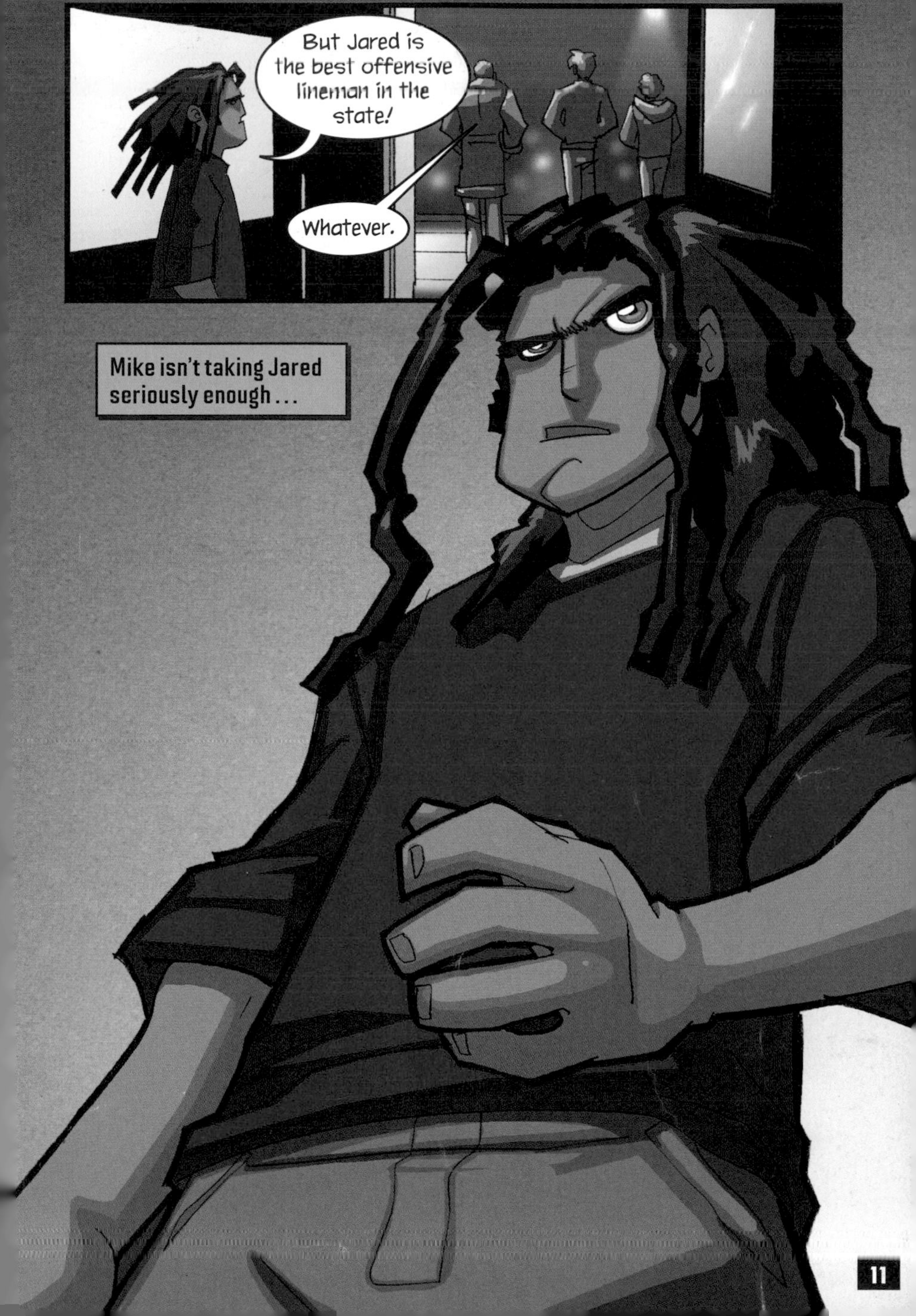
But Jared is the best offensive lineman in the state!
Whatever.
Mike isn't taking Jared seriously enough . . .

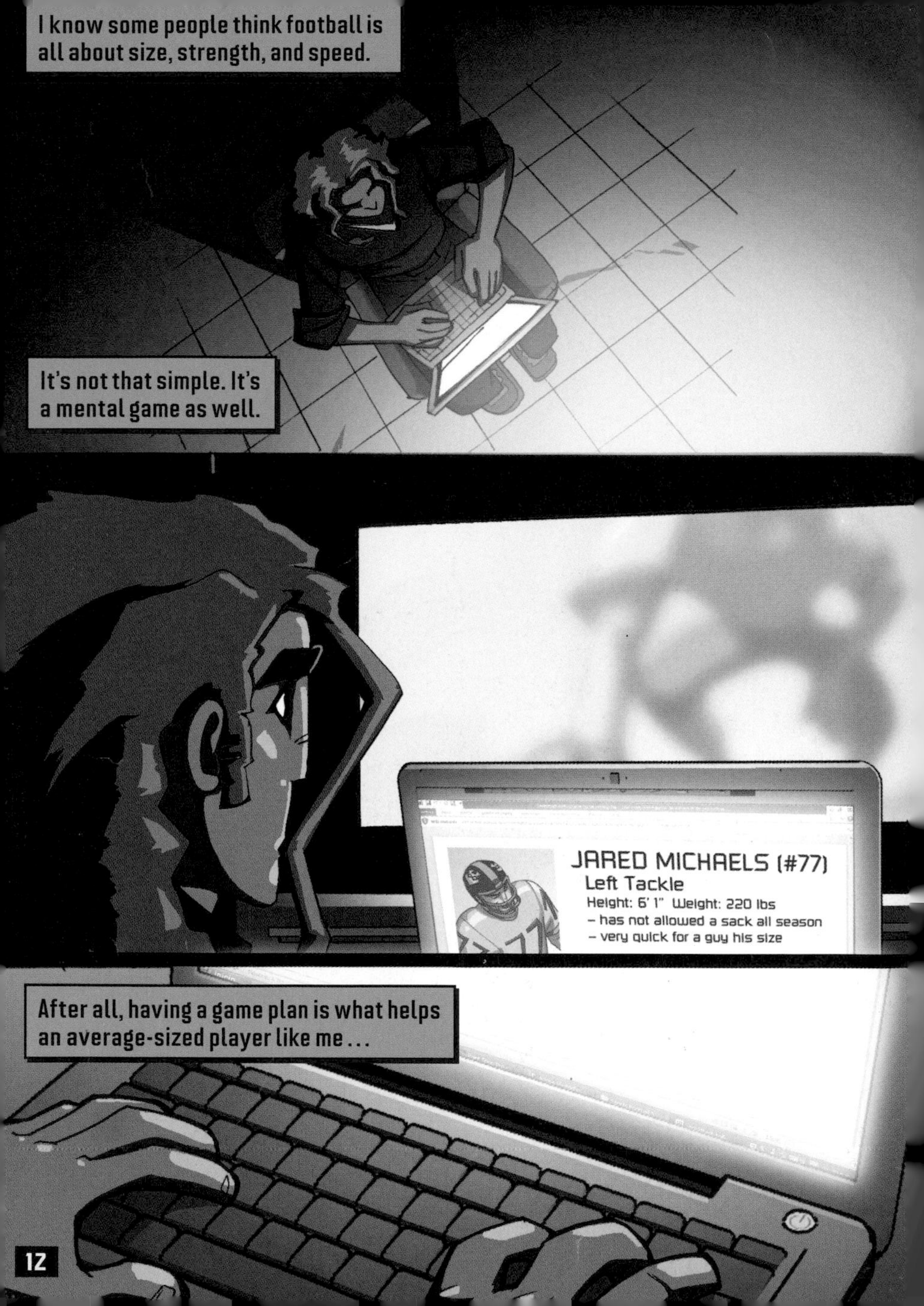

I know some people think football is all about size, strength, and speed.
It's not that simple. It's a mental game as well.
JARED MICHAELS (#77)
Left Tackle
Height: 6' 1" Weight: 220 lbs
– has not allowed a sack all season
– very quick for a guy his size
After all, having a game plan is what helps an average-sized player like me . . .

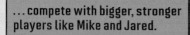
...compete with bigger, stronger players like Mike and Jared.

CLICK

It's a sweep outside!

Jared Michaels leads the blocking for a big rushing gain!

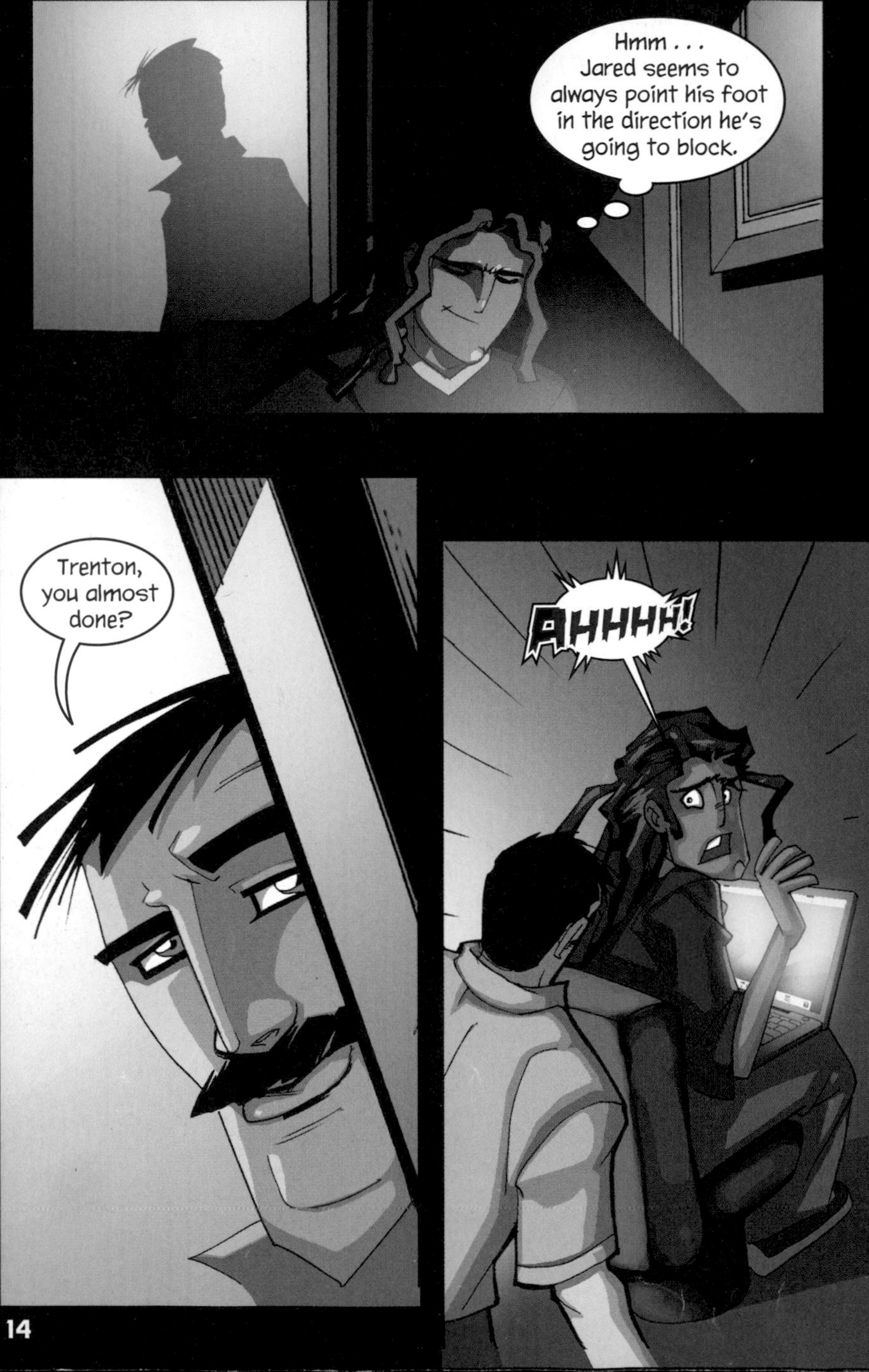
Hmm . . . Jared seems to always point his foot in the direction he's going to block.
Trenton, you almost done?
AHHHH!

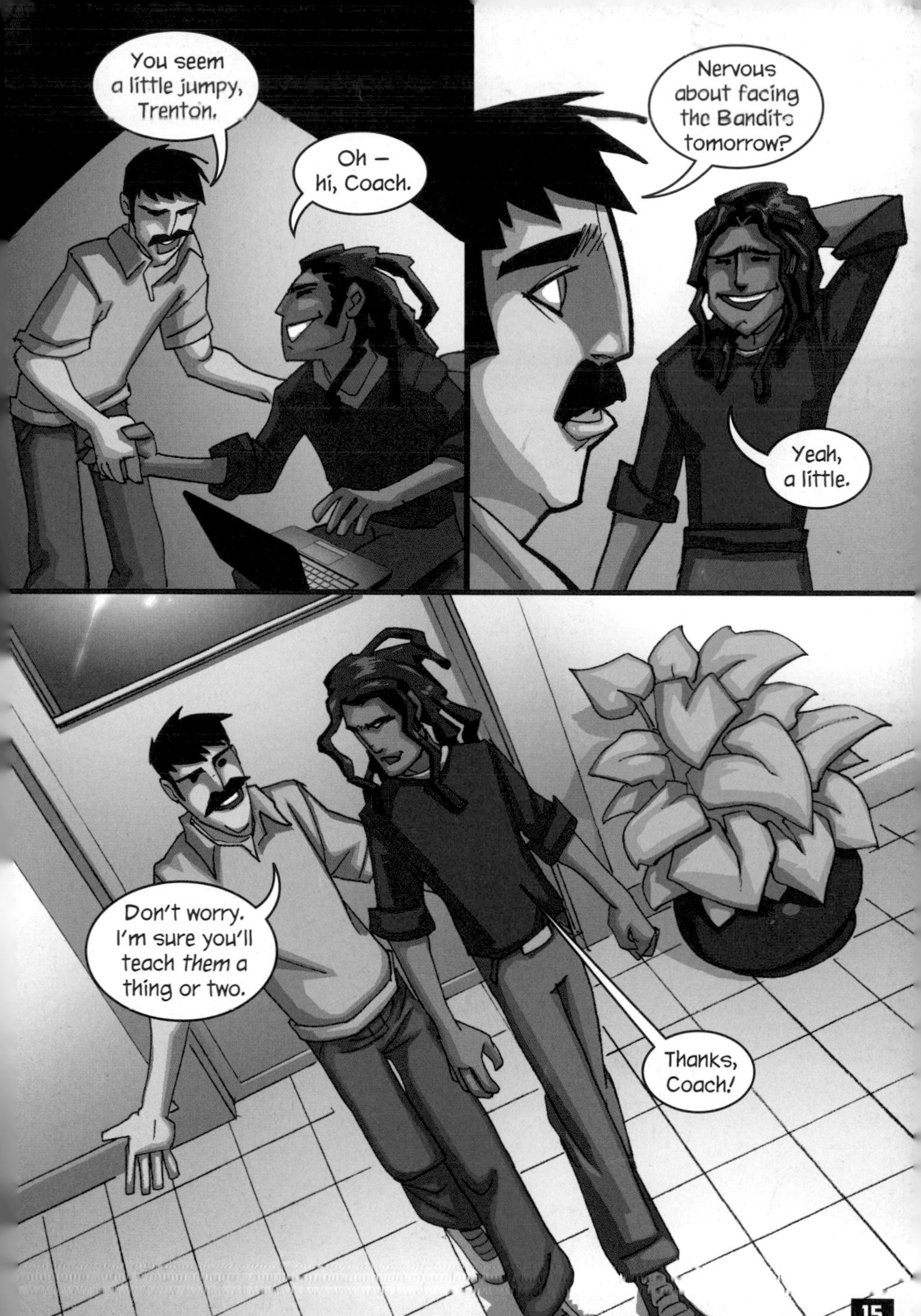
You seem a little jumpy, Trenton.
Oh — hi, Coach.
Nervous about facing the Bandits tomorrow?
Yeah, a little.
Don't worry. I'm sure you'll teach *them* a thing or two.
Thanks, Coach!

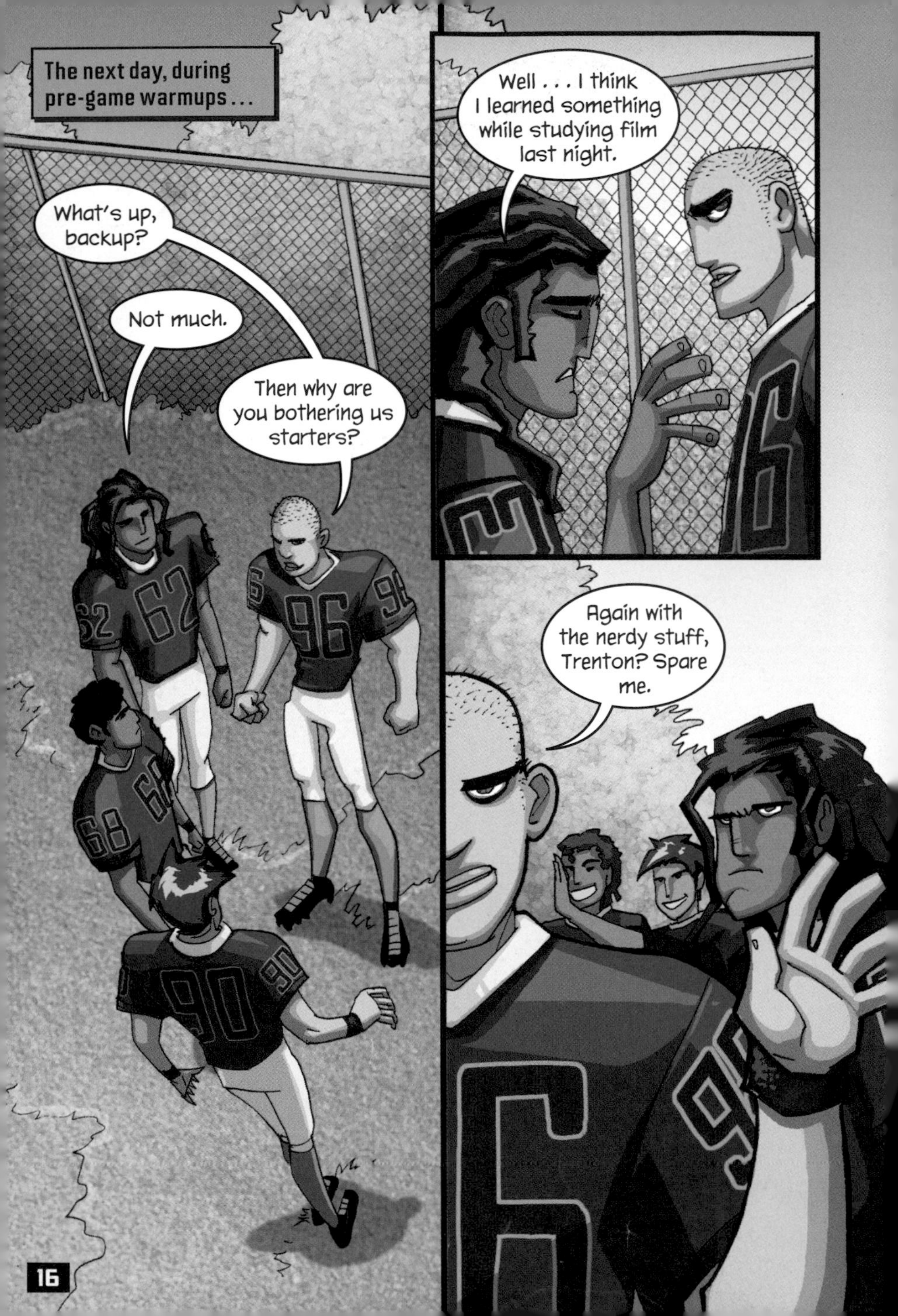
The next day, during pre-game warmups . . .
What's up, backup?
Not much.
Then why are you bothering us starters?
Well . . . I think I learned something while studying film last night.
Again with the nerdy stuff, Trenton? Spare me.

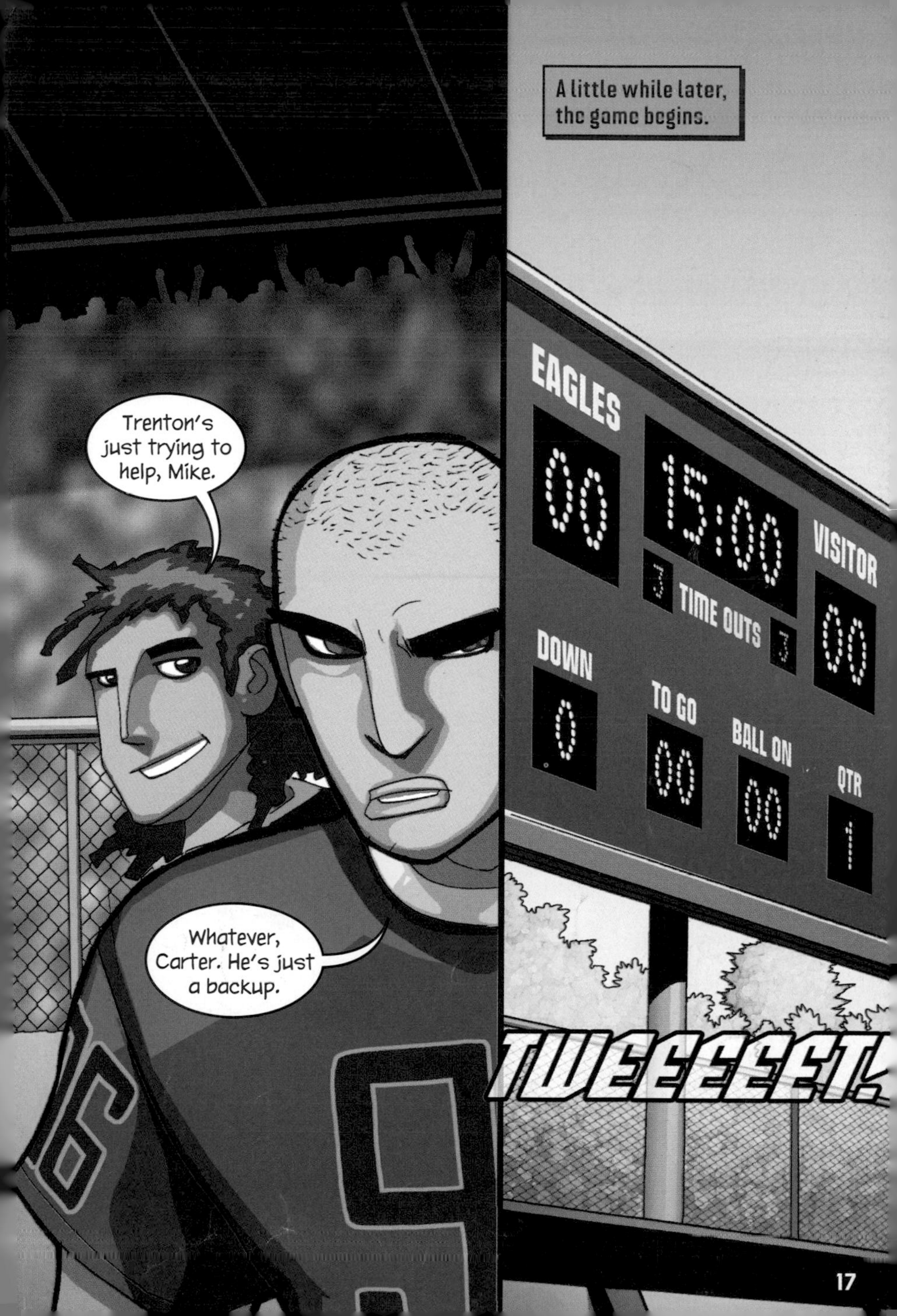
Trenton's just trying to help, Mike.
Whatever, Carter. He's just a backup.
A little while later, the game begins.
EAGLES
00
15:00
3
TIME OUTS
3
VISITOR
00
DOWN
0
TO GO
00
BALL ON
00
QTR
1
TWEEEEET!

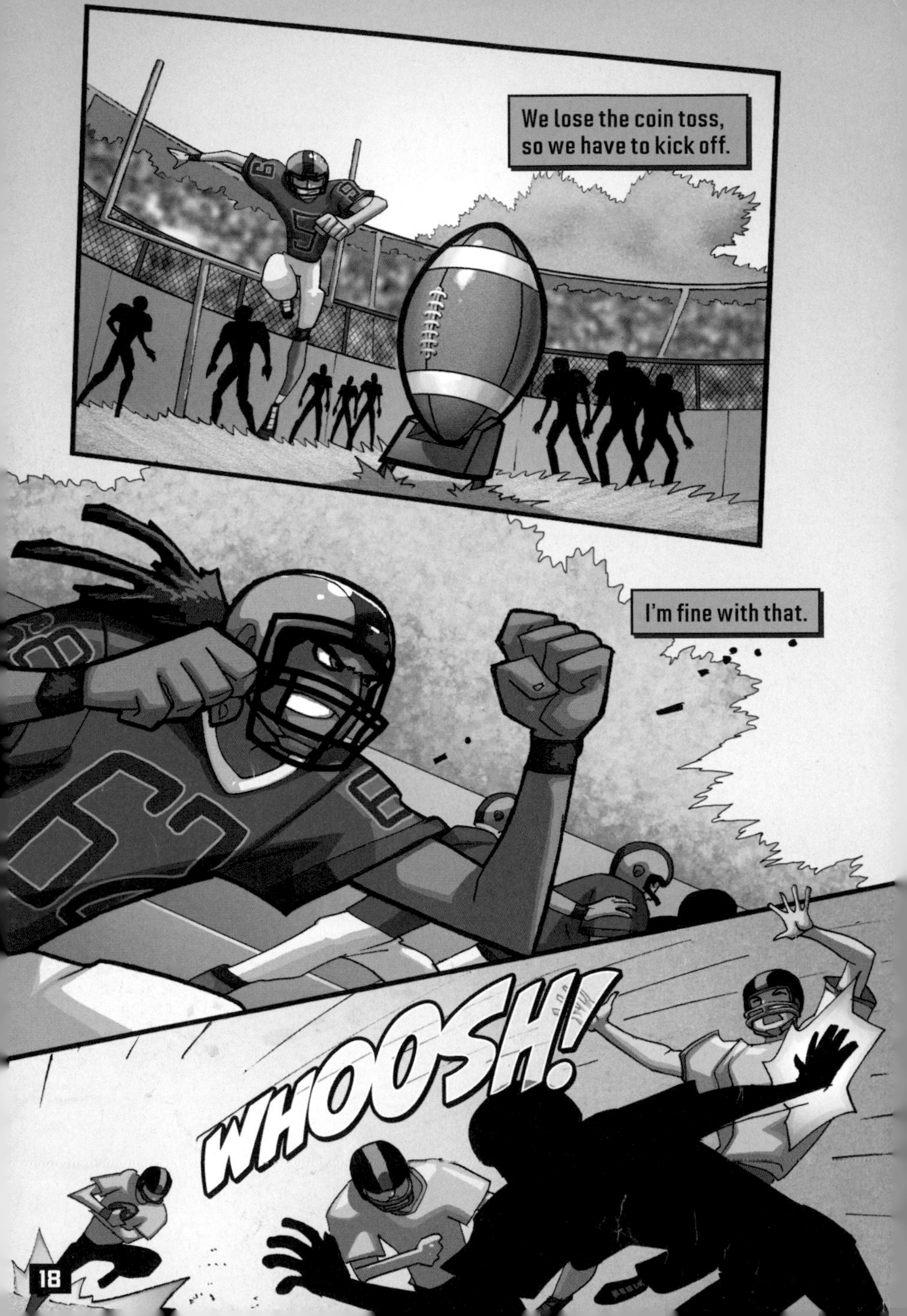
We lose the coin toss, so we have to kick off.
I'm fine with that.
WHOOSH!

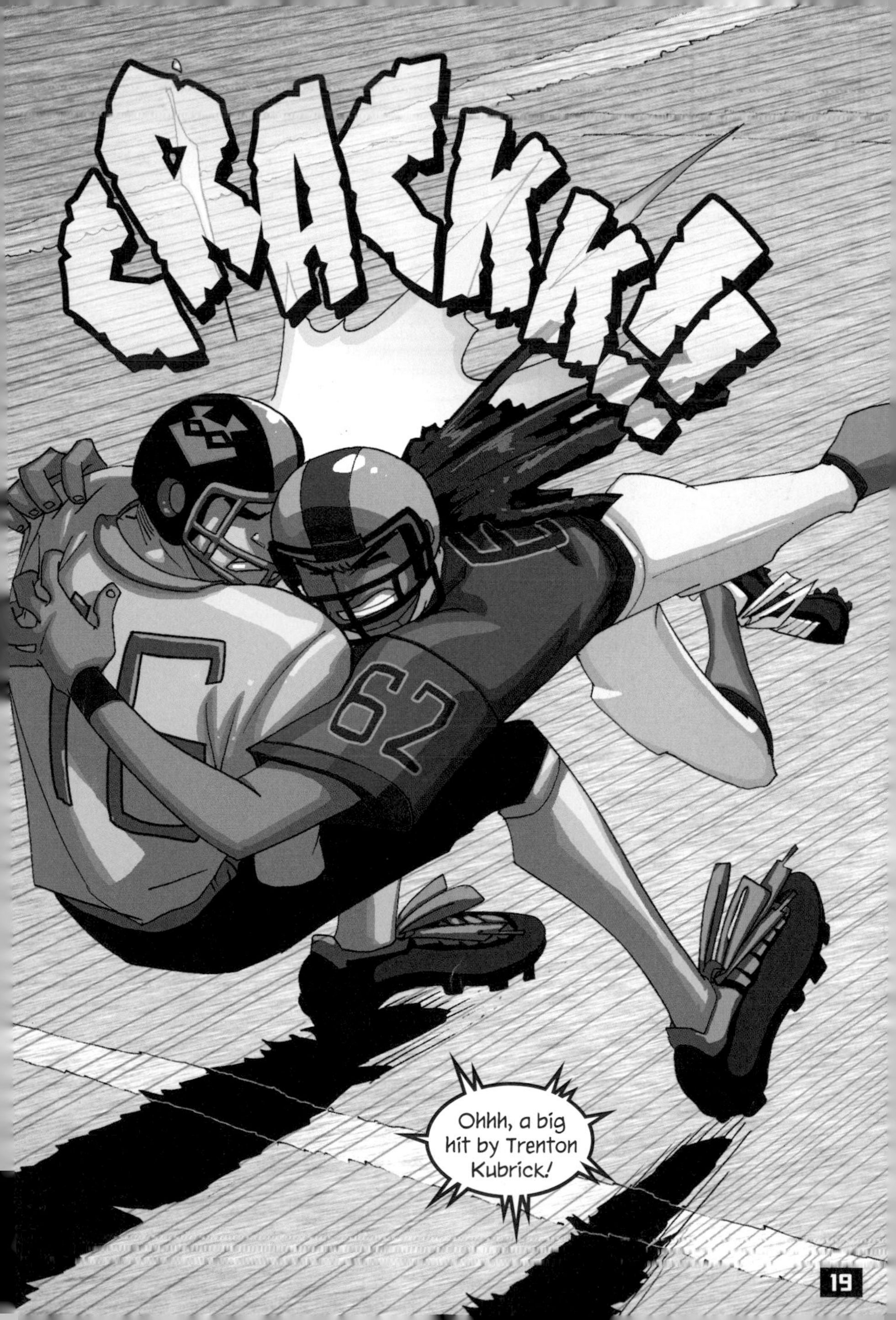
CRACK!!
Ohhh, a big hit by Trenton Kubrick!

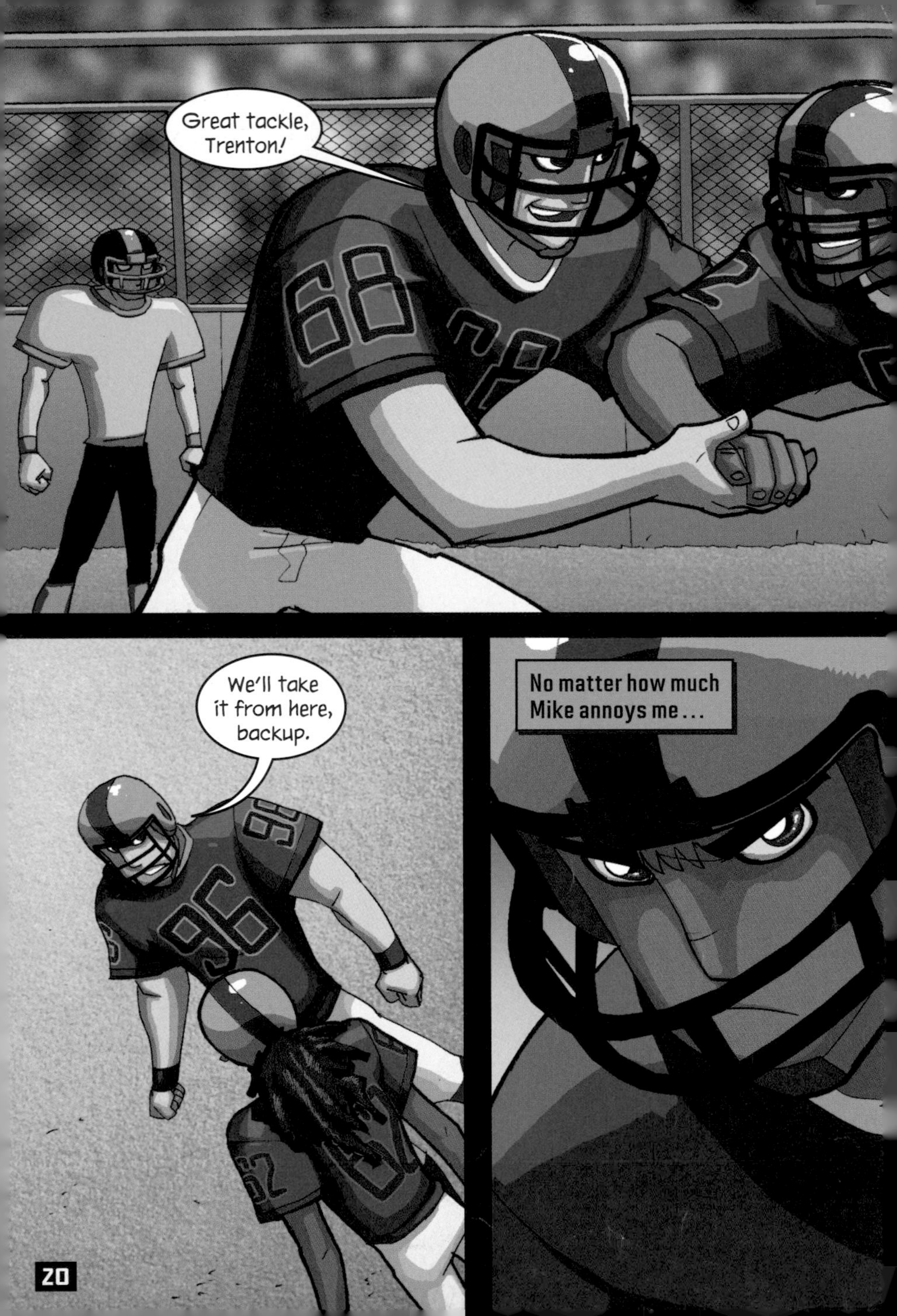
Great tackle, Trenton!
We'll take it from here, backup.
No matter how much Mike annoys me . . .

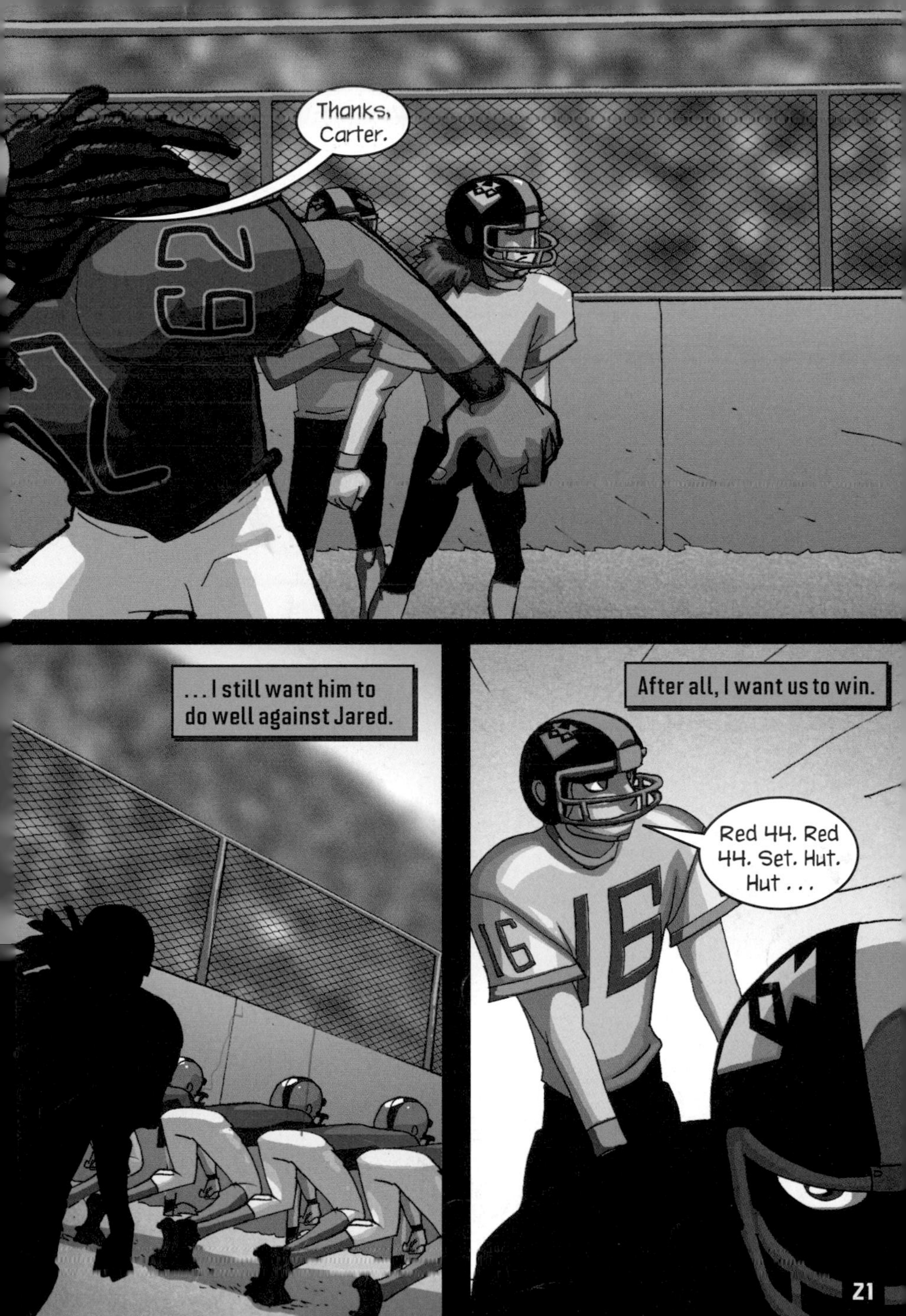
Thanks, Carter.
. . . I still want him to do well against Jared.
After all, I want us to win.
Red 44. Red 44. Set. Hut. Hut . . .

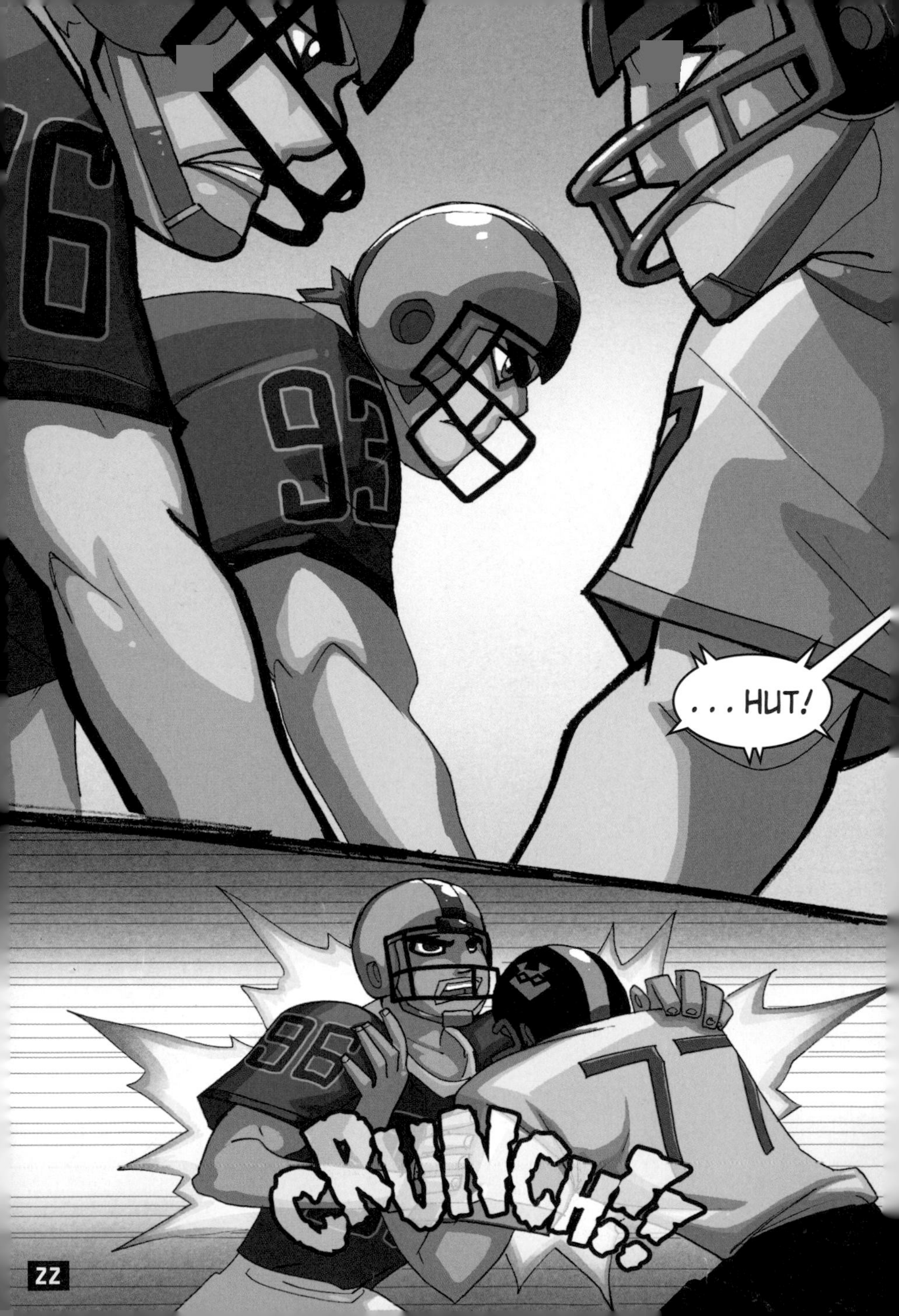
. . . HUT!
CRUNCH!!

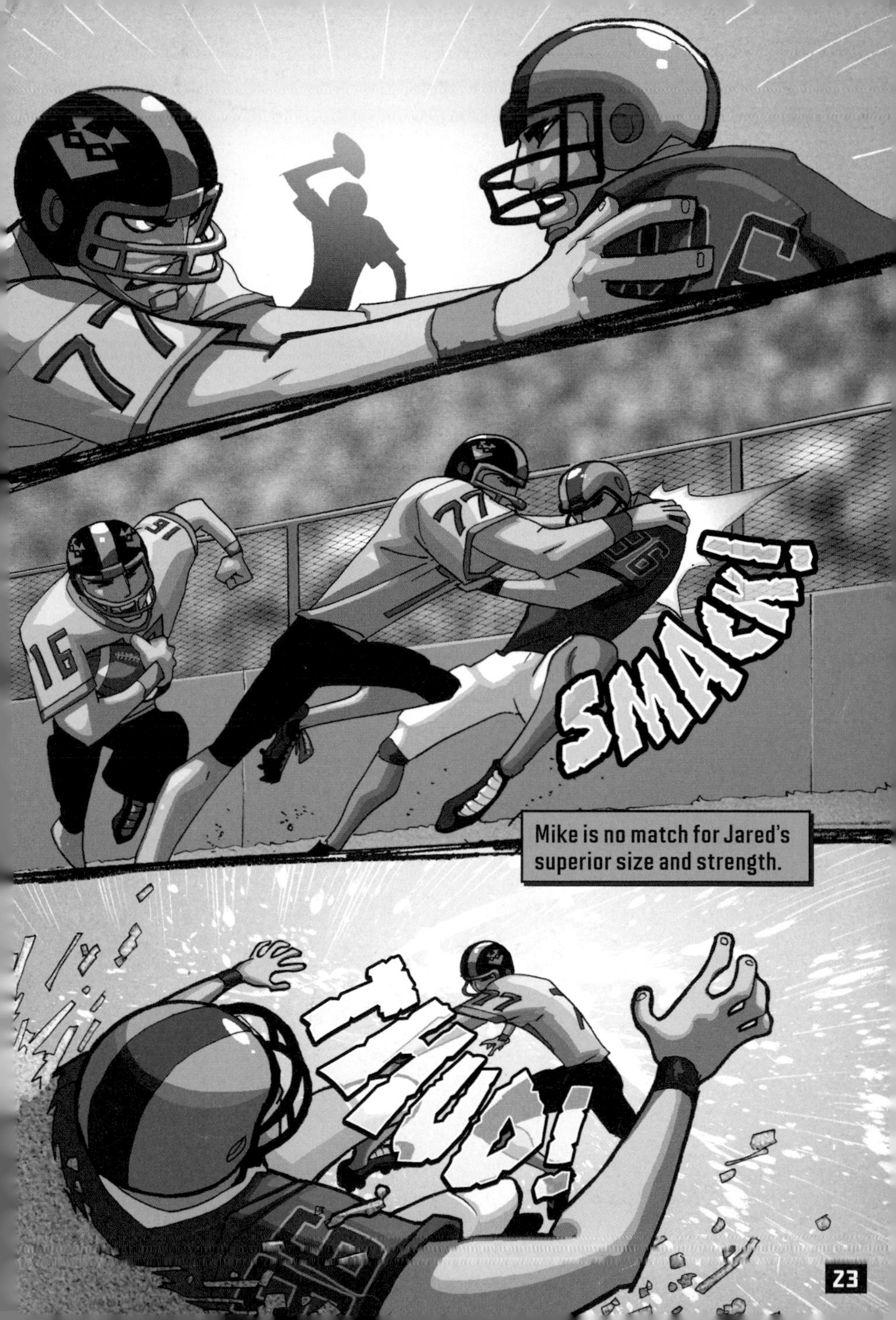
SMACK!
Mike is no match for Jared's superior size and strength.
THUD!

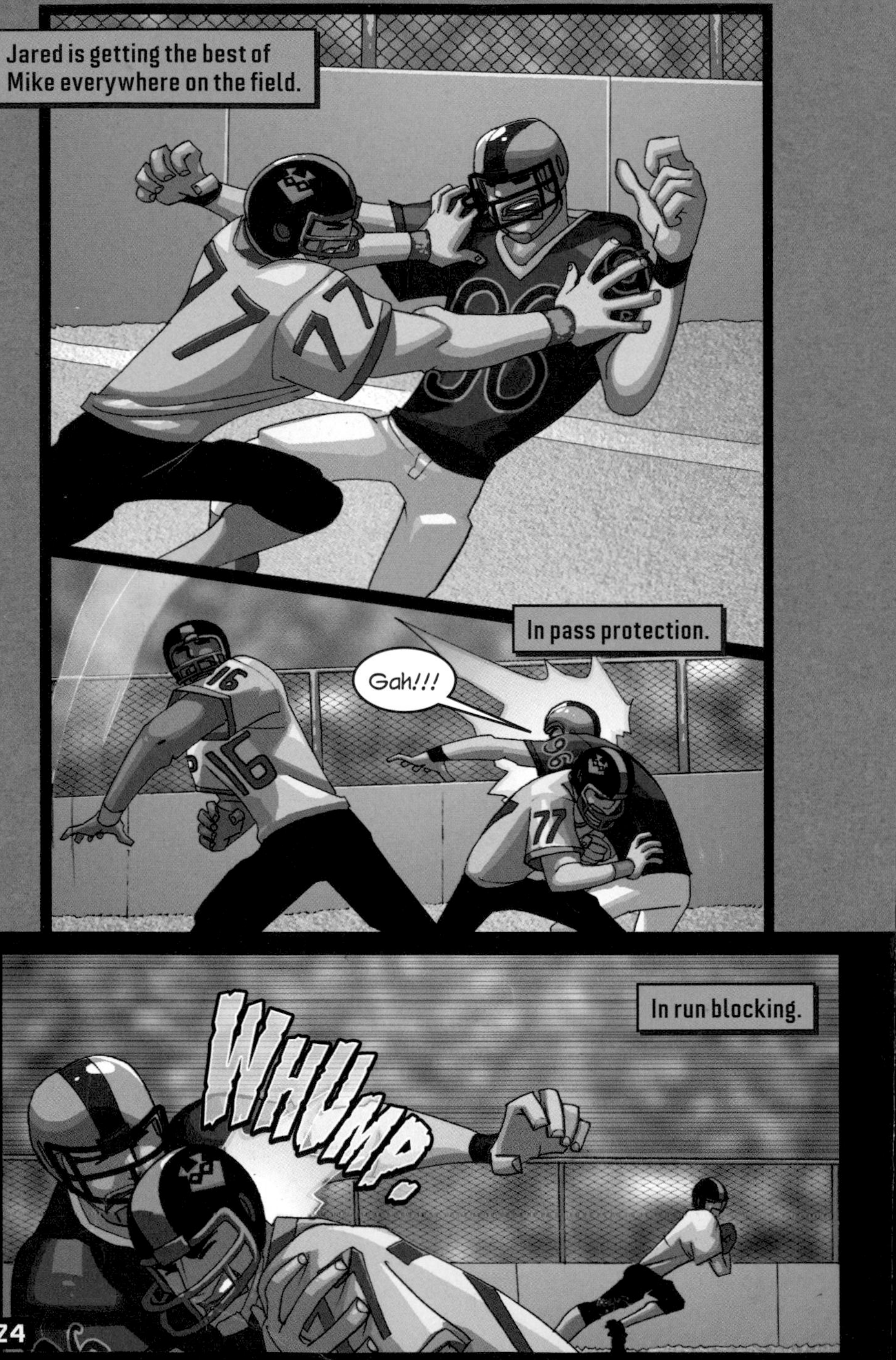

Jared is getting the best of Mike everywhere on the field.
In pass protection.
Gah!!!
In run blocking.
WHUMP!

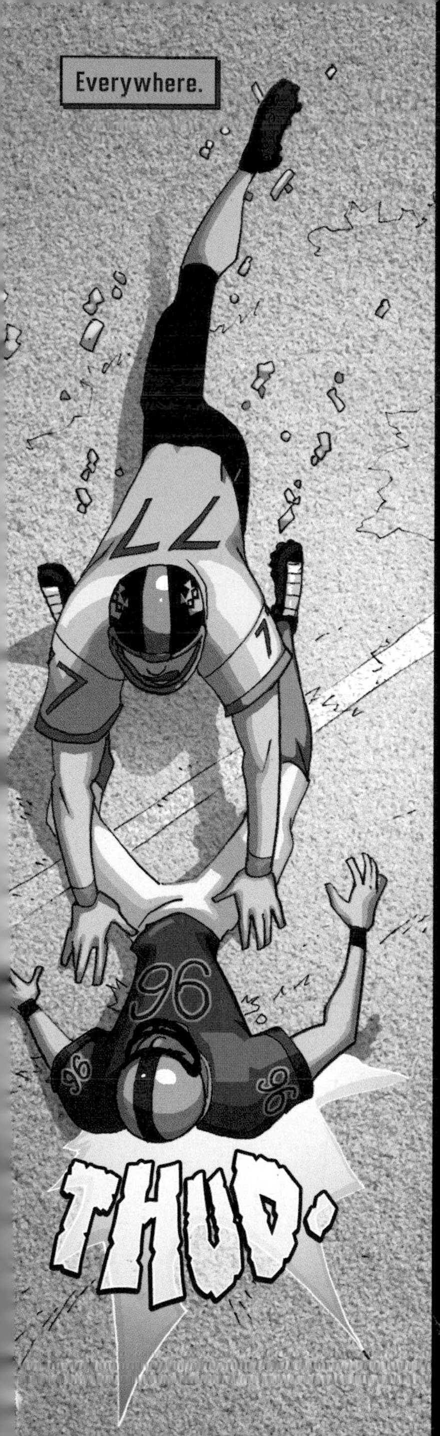
Everywhere.
THUD.

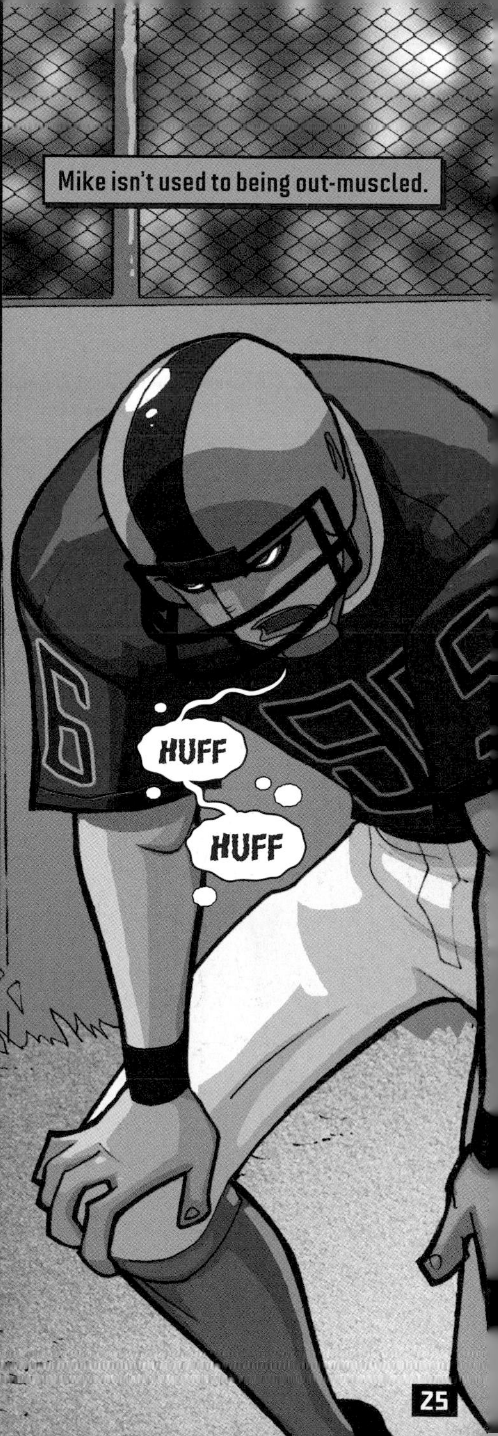
Mike isn't used to being out-muscled.
HUFF
HUFF

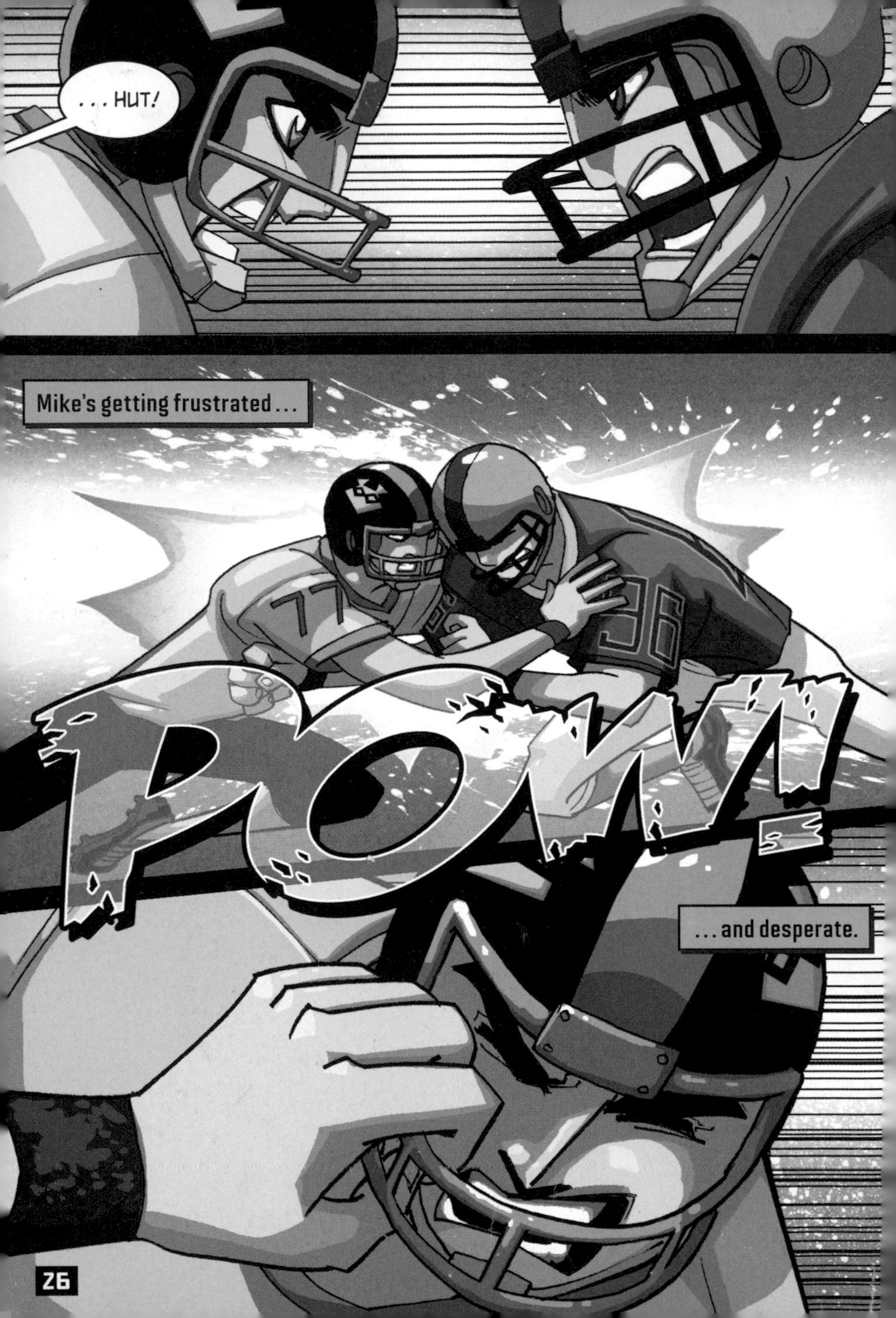
. . . HUT!
Mike's getting frustrated . . .
POW!
. . . and desperate.

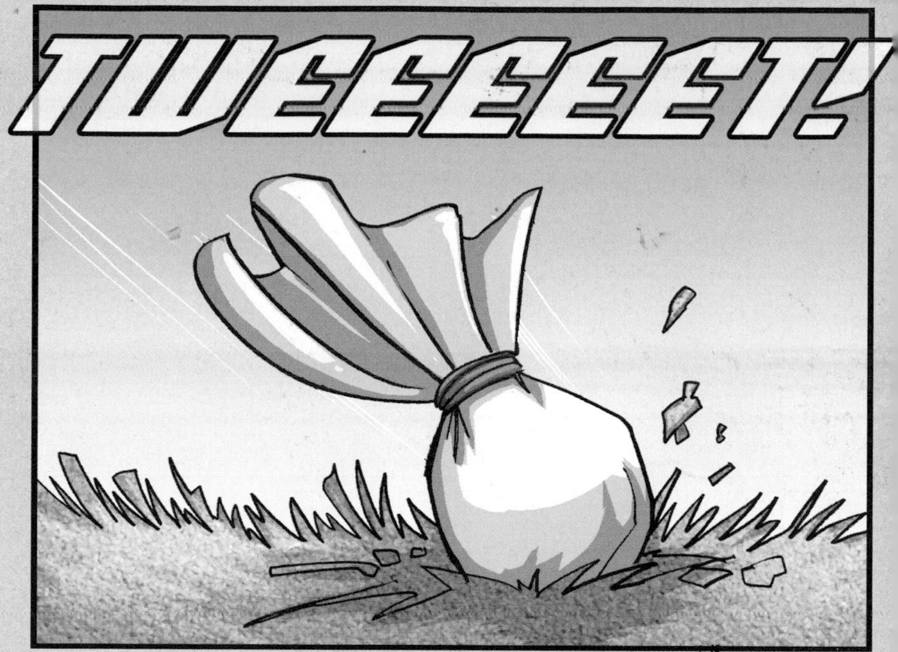
TWEEEEET!

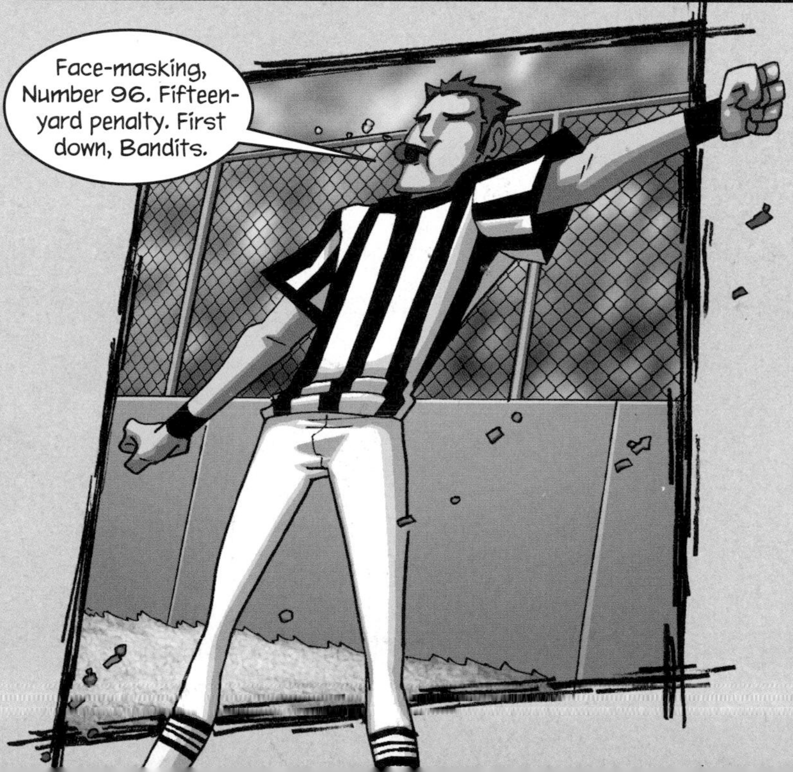
Face-masking, Number 96. Fifteen-yard penalty. First down, Bandits.

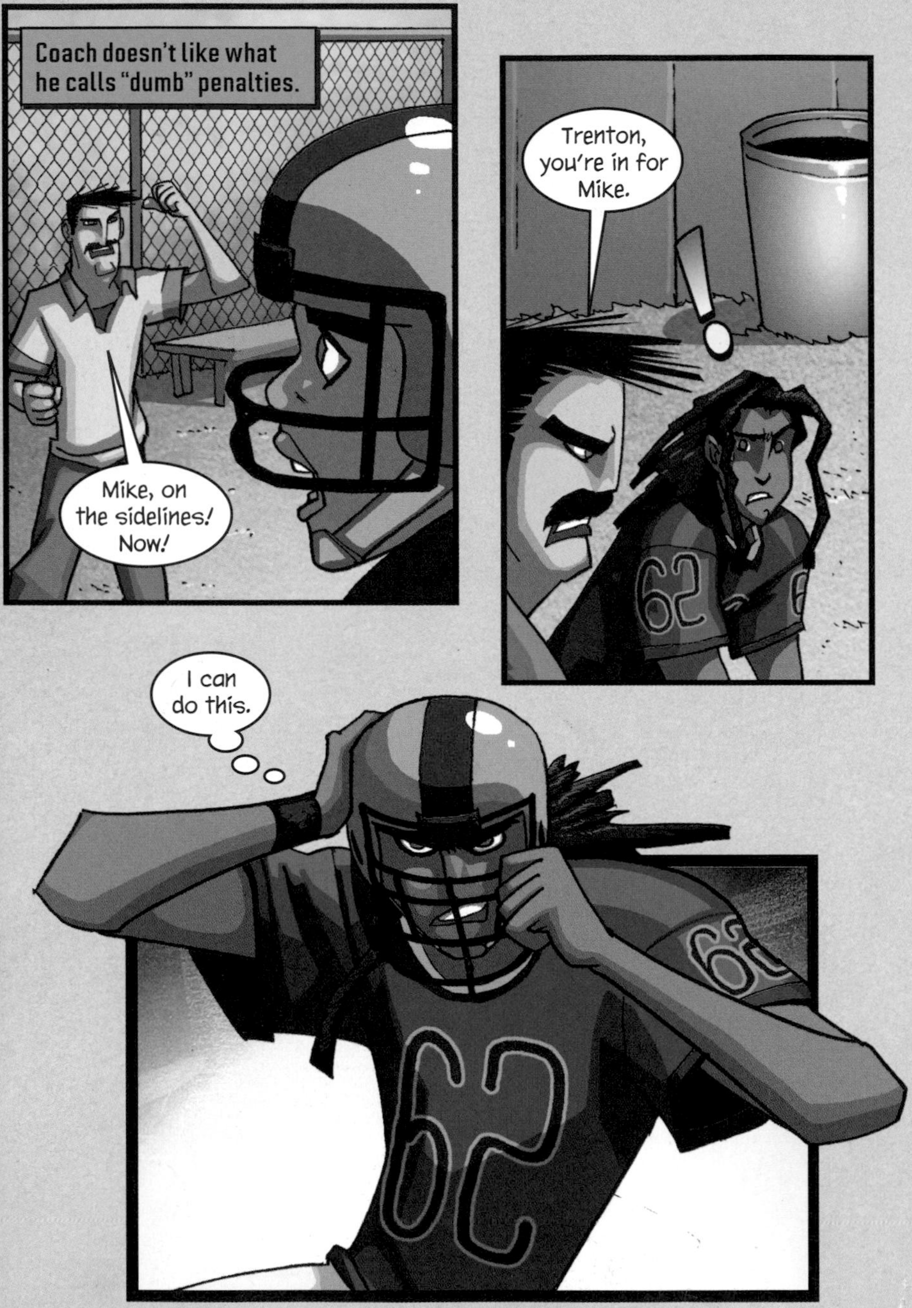
Coach doesn't like what he calls "dumb" penalties.
Mike, on the sidelines! Now!
Trenton, you're in for Mike.
!
I can do this.

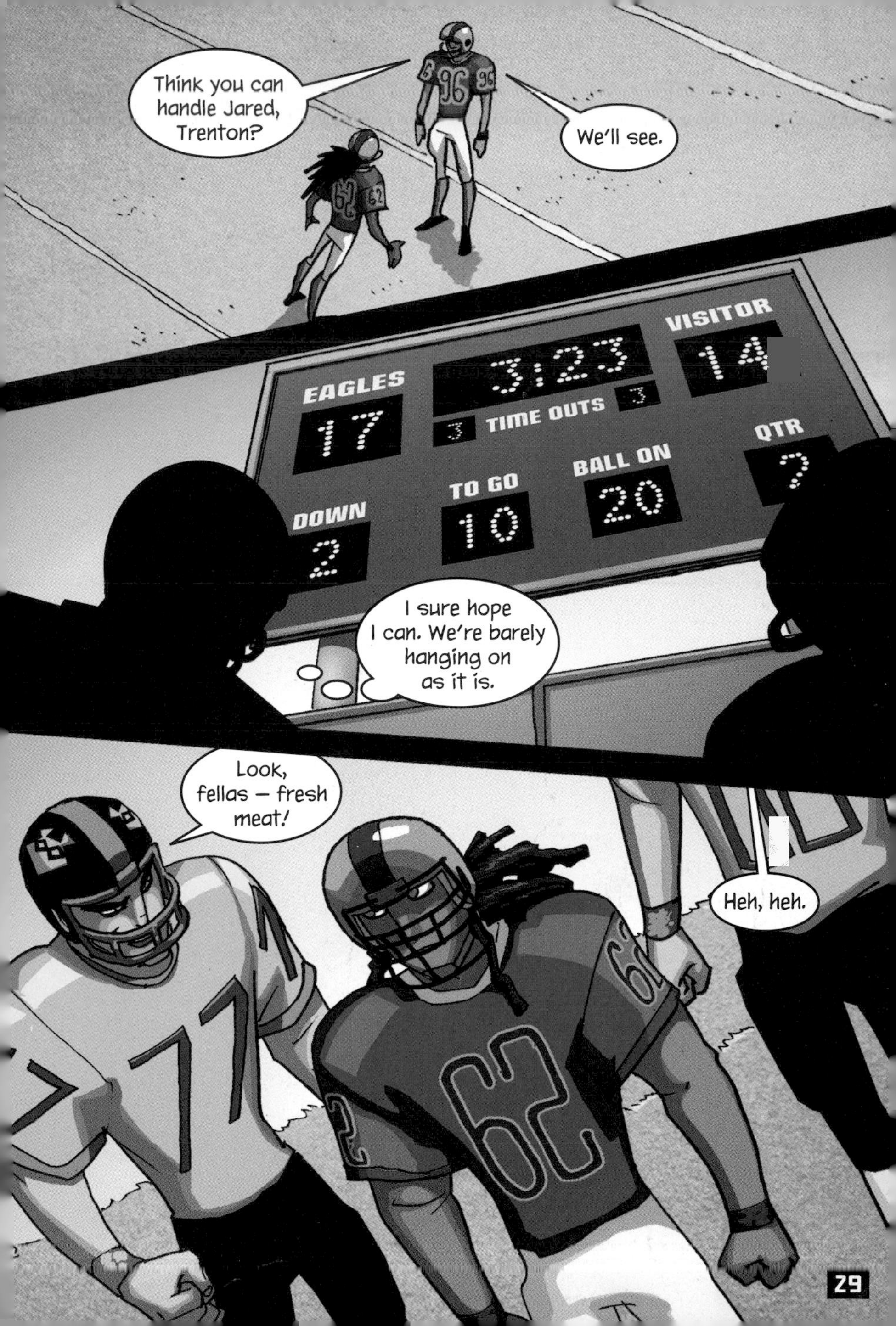
Think you can handle Jared, Trenton?
We'll see.
EAGLES
17
3:23
VISITOR
14
TIME OUTS
3
3
QTR
BALL ON
20
TO GO
10
DOWN
2
I sure hope I can. We're barely hanging on as it is.
Look, fellas — fresh meat!
Heh, heh.

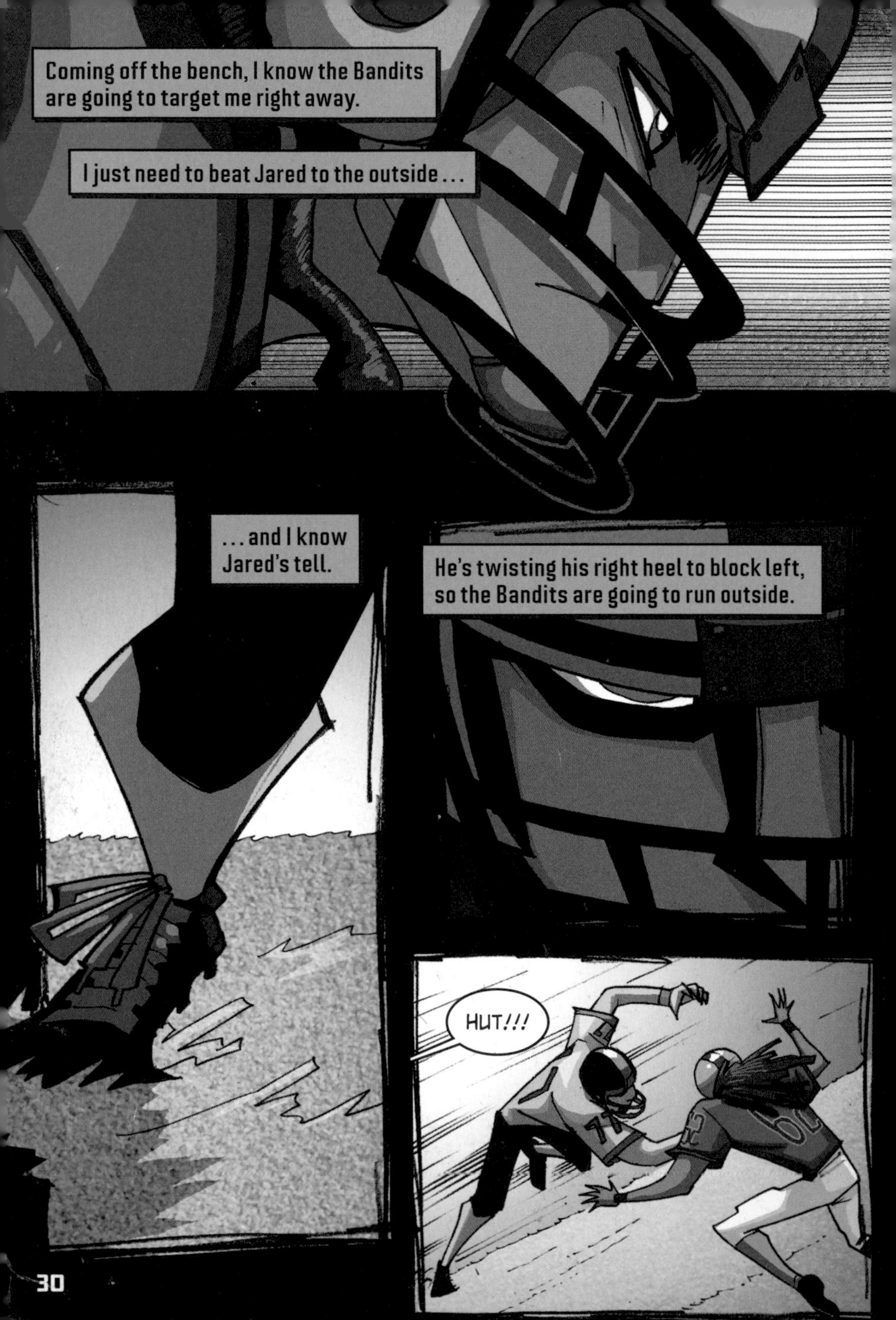
Coming off the bench, I know the Bandits are going to target me right away.
I just need to beat Jared to the outside . . .
. . . and I know Jared's tell.
He's twisting his right heel to block left, so the Bandits are going to run outside.
HUT!!!

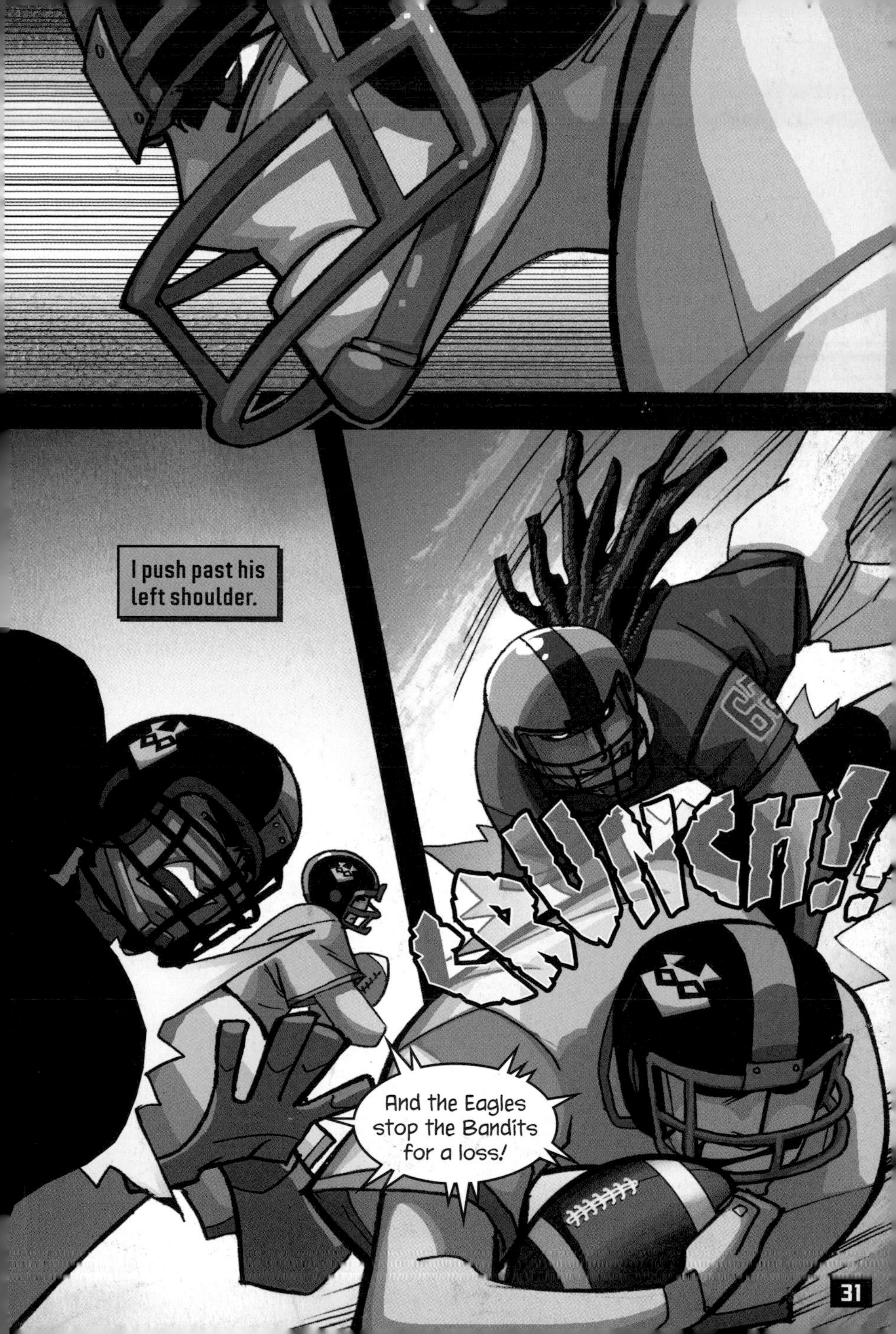
I push past his left shoulder.
CRUNCH!!
And the Eagles stop the Bandits for a loss!

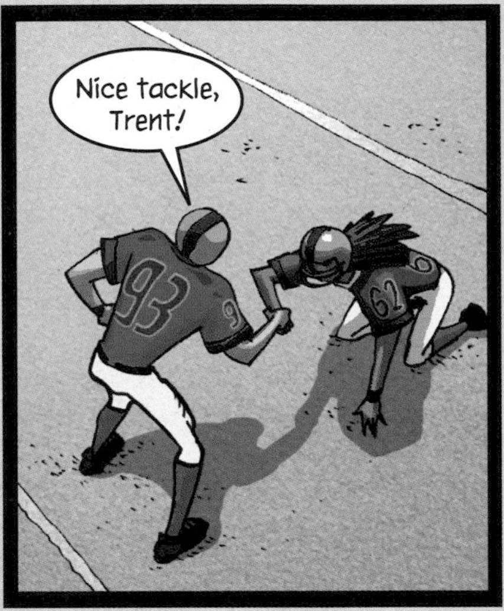
Nice tackle, Trent!

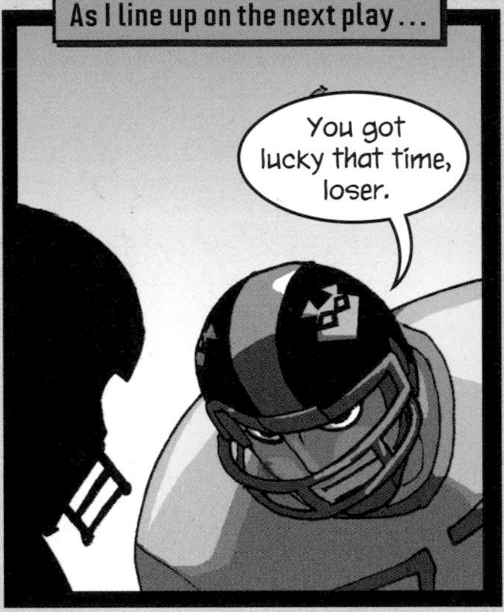
As I line up on the next play . . .
You got lucky that time, loser.

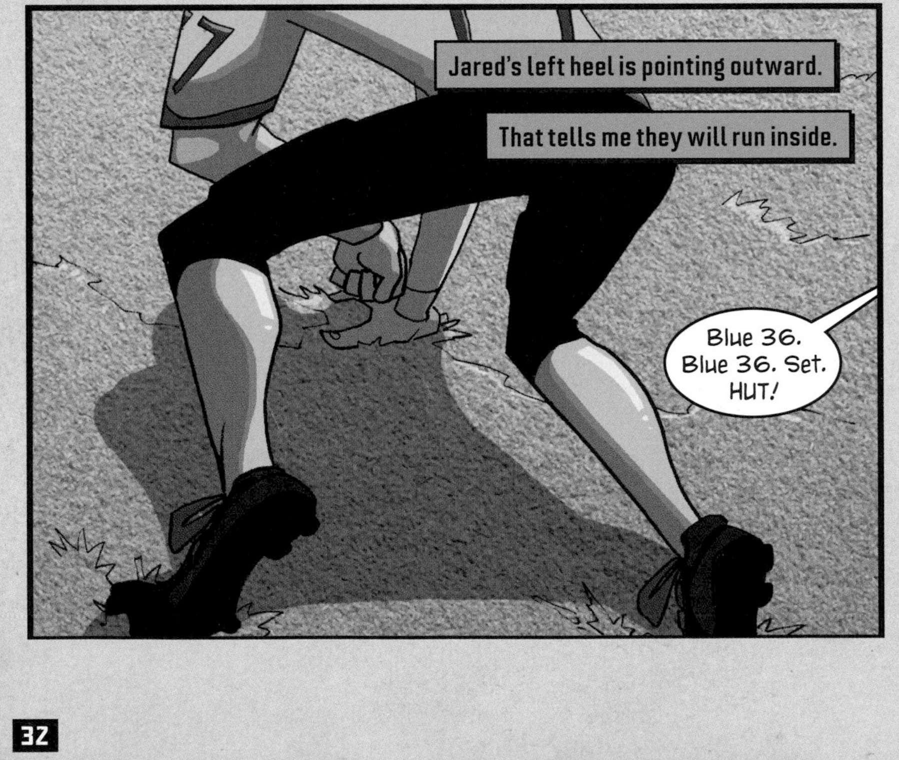
Jared's left heel is pointing outward.
That tells me they will run inside.
Blue 36. Blue 36. Set. HUT!

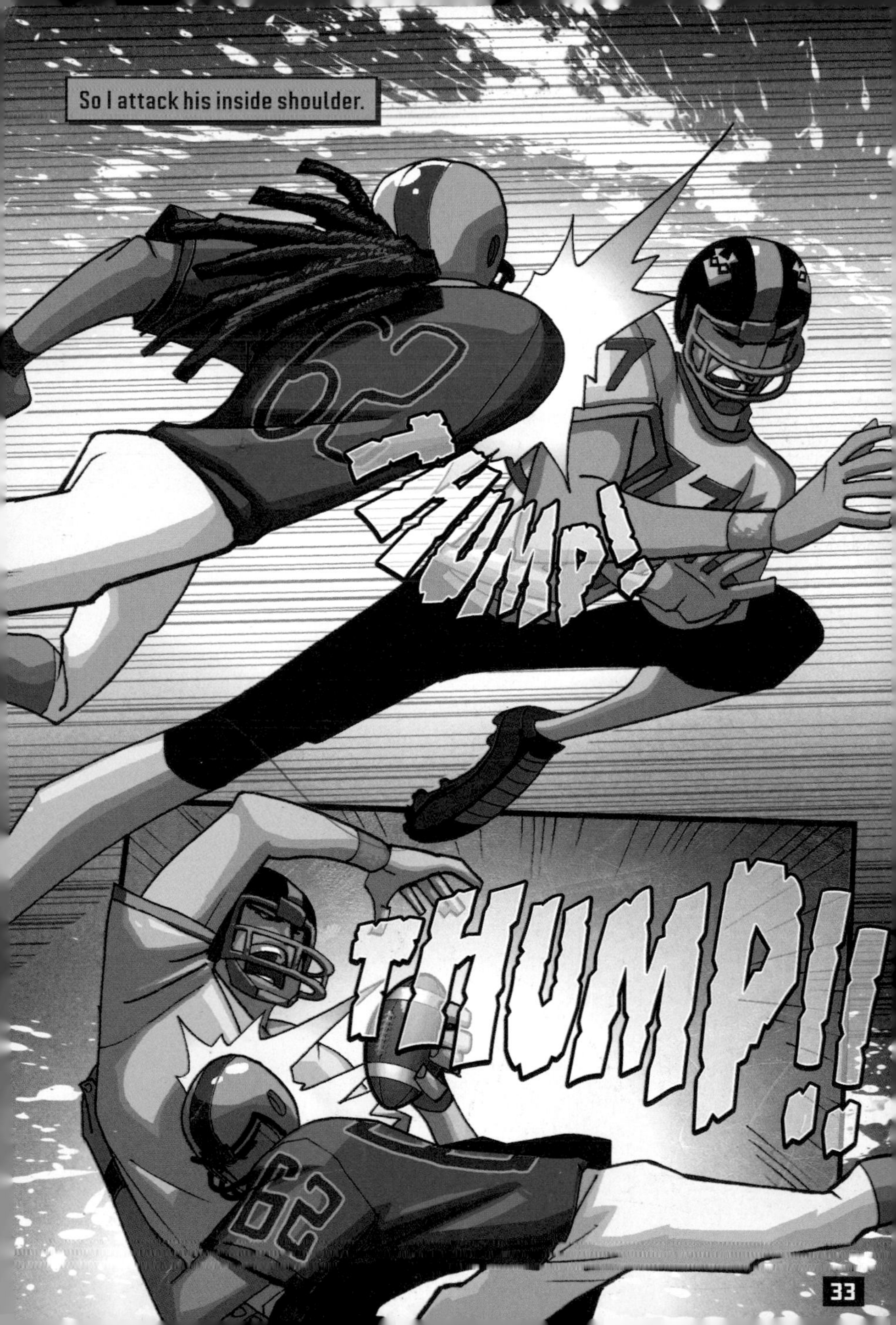
So I attack his inside shoulder.
THUMP!
THUMP!!

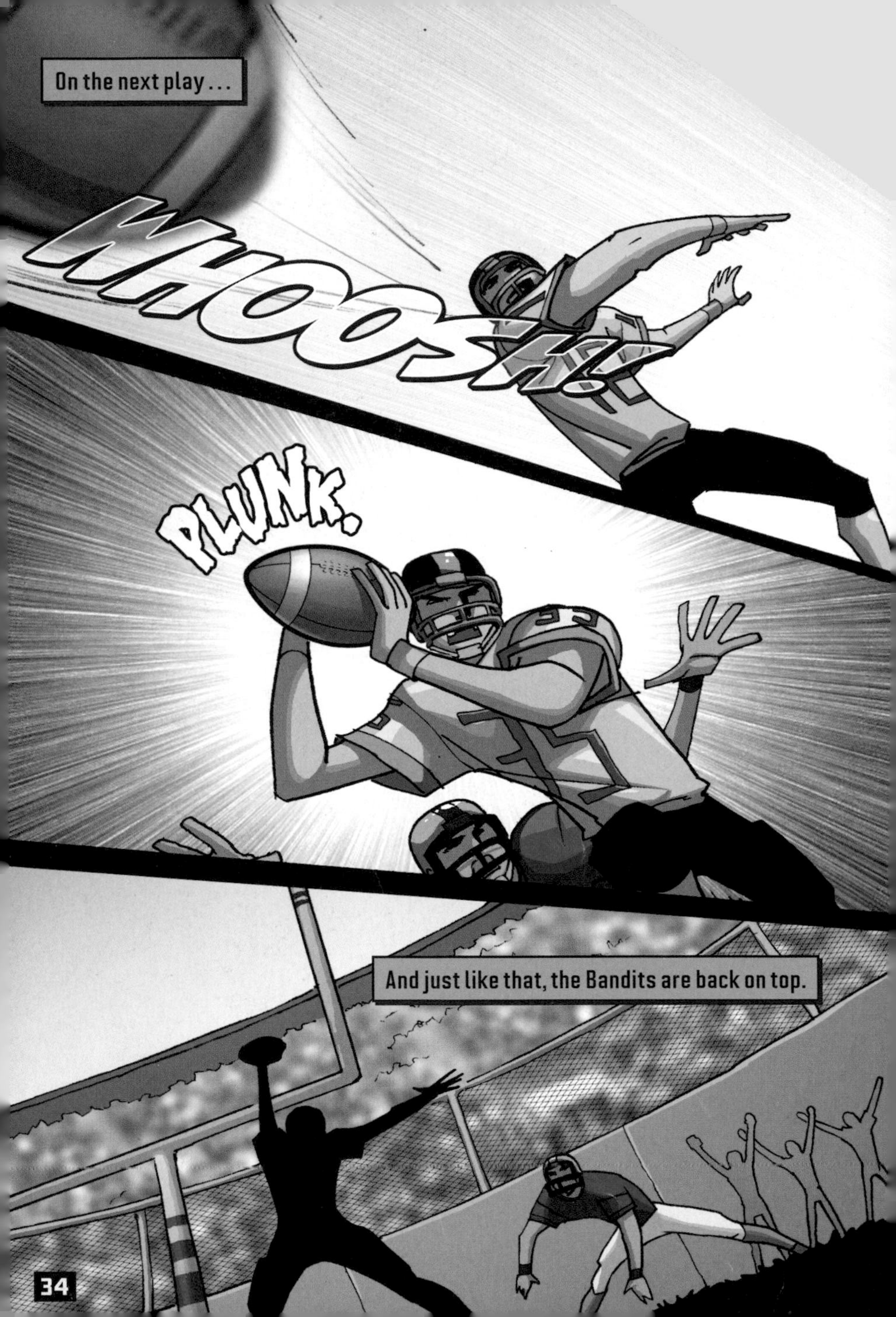
On the next play . . .
WHOOSH!
PLUNK!
And just like that, the Bandits are back on top.

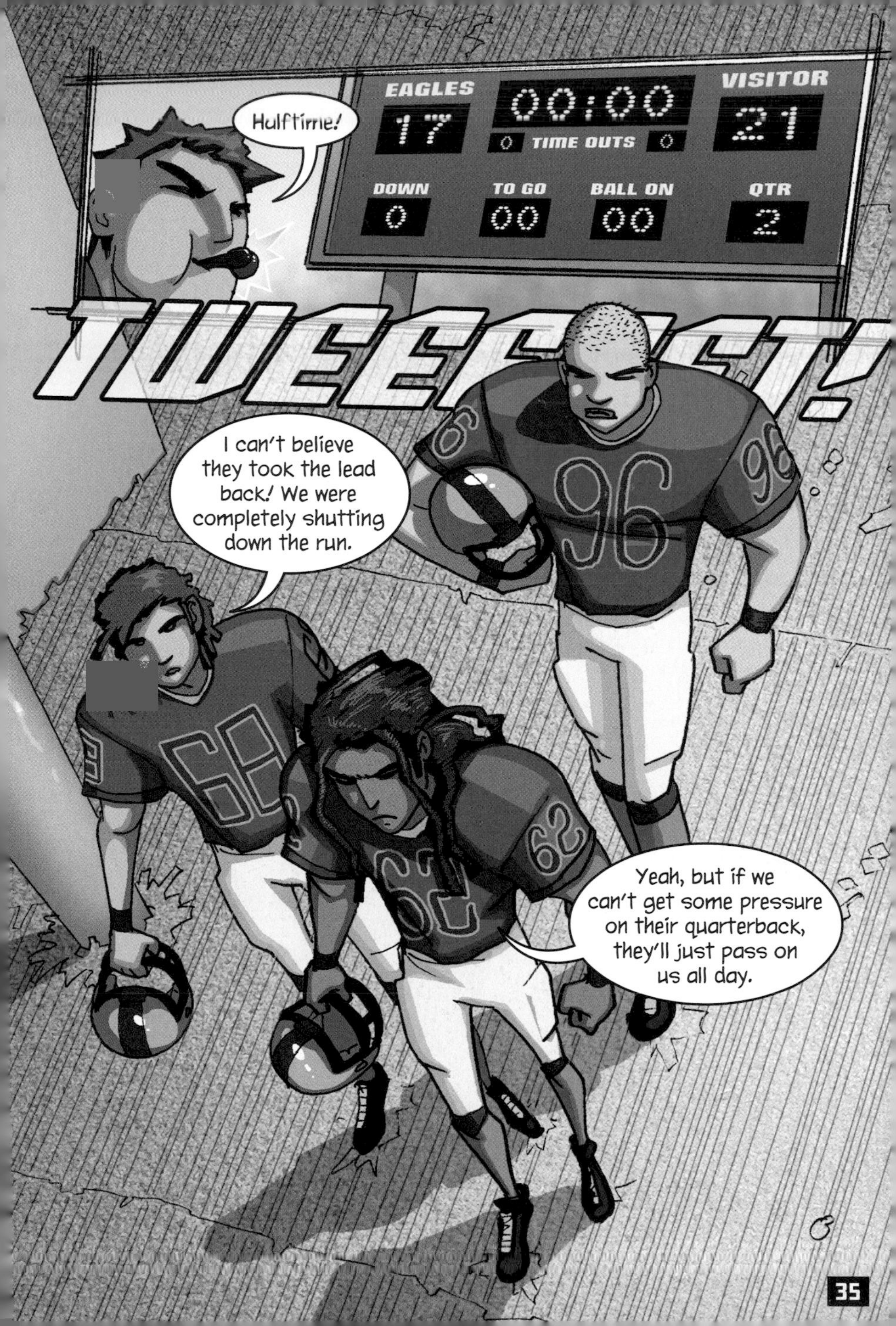
EAGLES
17
00:00
0 TIME OUTS 0
VISITOR
21
DOWN
0
TO GO
00
BALL ON
00
QTR
2
Halftime!
TWEEEEET!
I can't believe they took the lead back! We were completely shutting down the run.
Yeah, but if we can't get some pressure on their quarterback, they'll just pass on us all day.

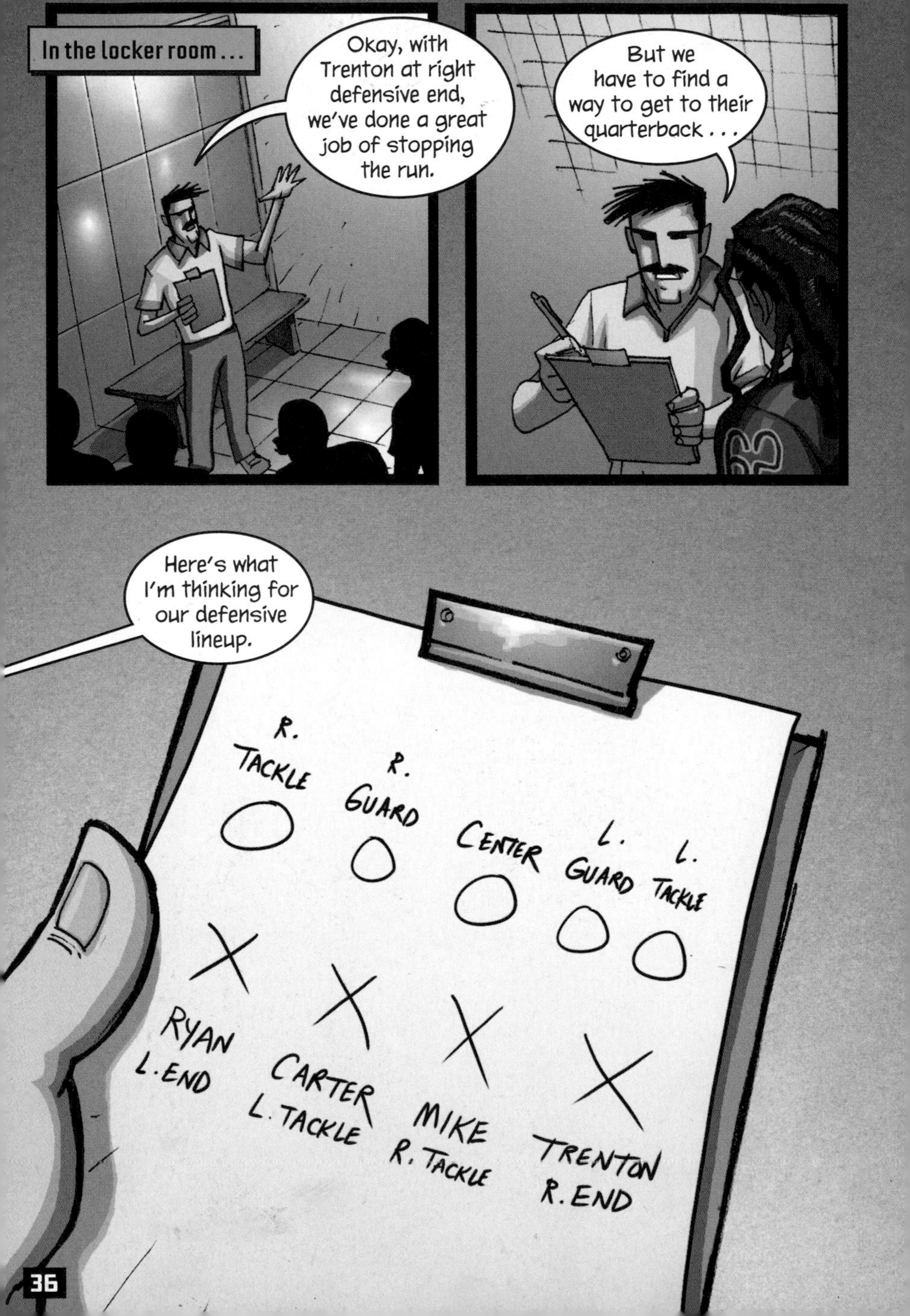
In the locker room . . .
Okay, with Trenton at right defensive end, we've done a great job of stopping the run.
But we have to find a way to get to their quarterback . . .
Here's what I'm thinking for our defensive lineup.
R. TACKLE
R. GUARD
CENTER
L. GUARD
L. TACKLE
RYAN L. END
CARTER L. TACKLE
MIKE R. TACKLE
TRENTON R. END

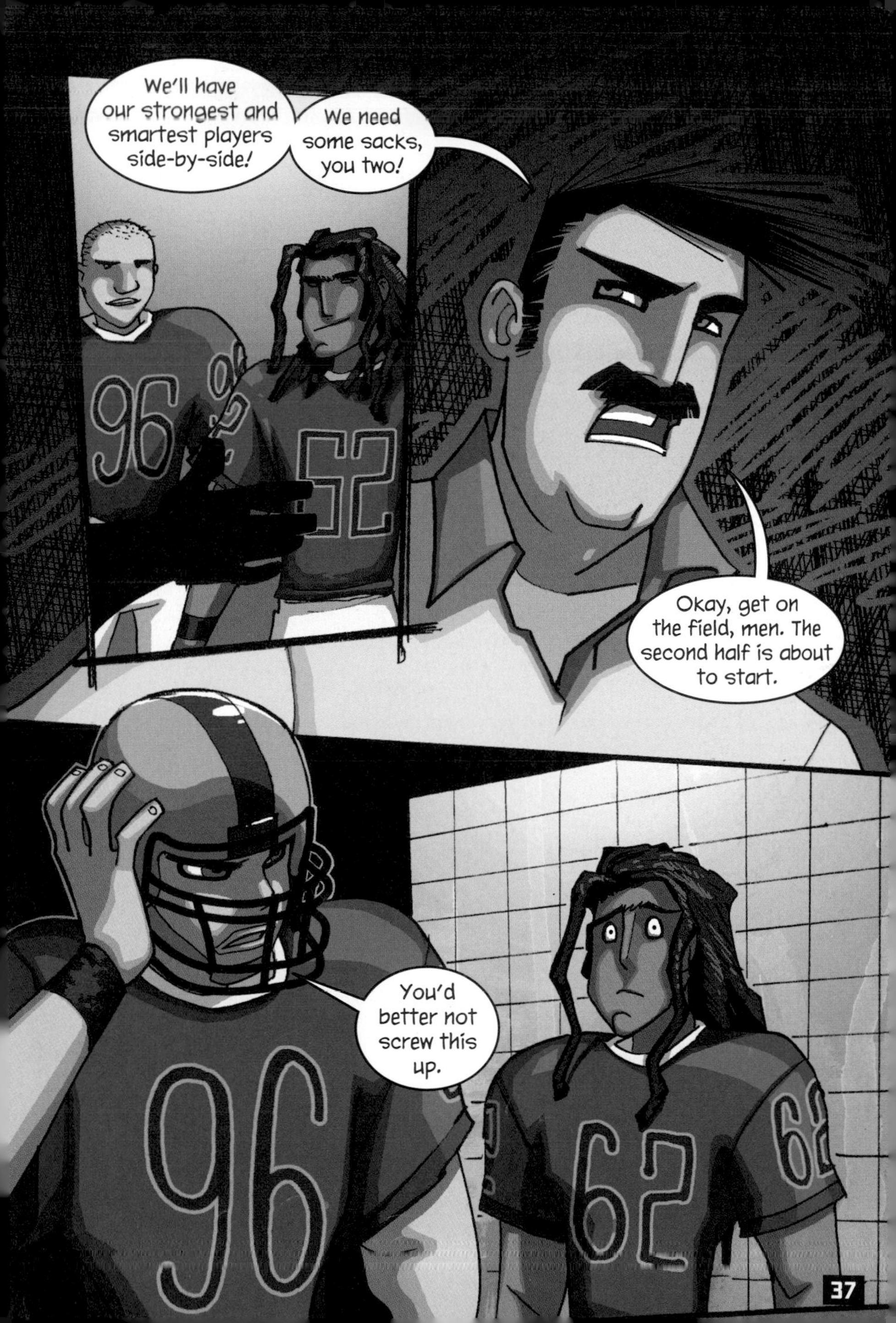
We'll have our strongest and smartest players side-by-side!
We need some sacks, you two!
Okay, get on the field, men. The second half is about to start.
You'd better not screw this up.

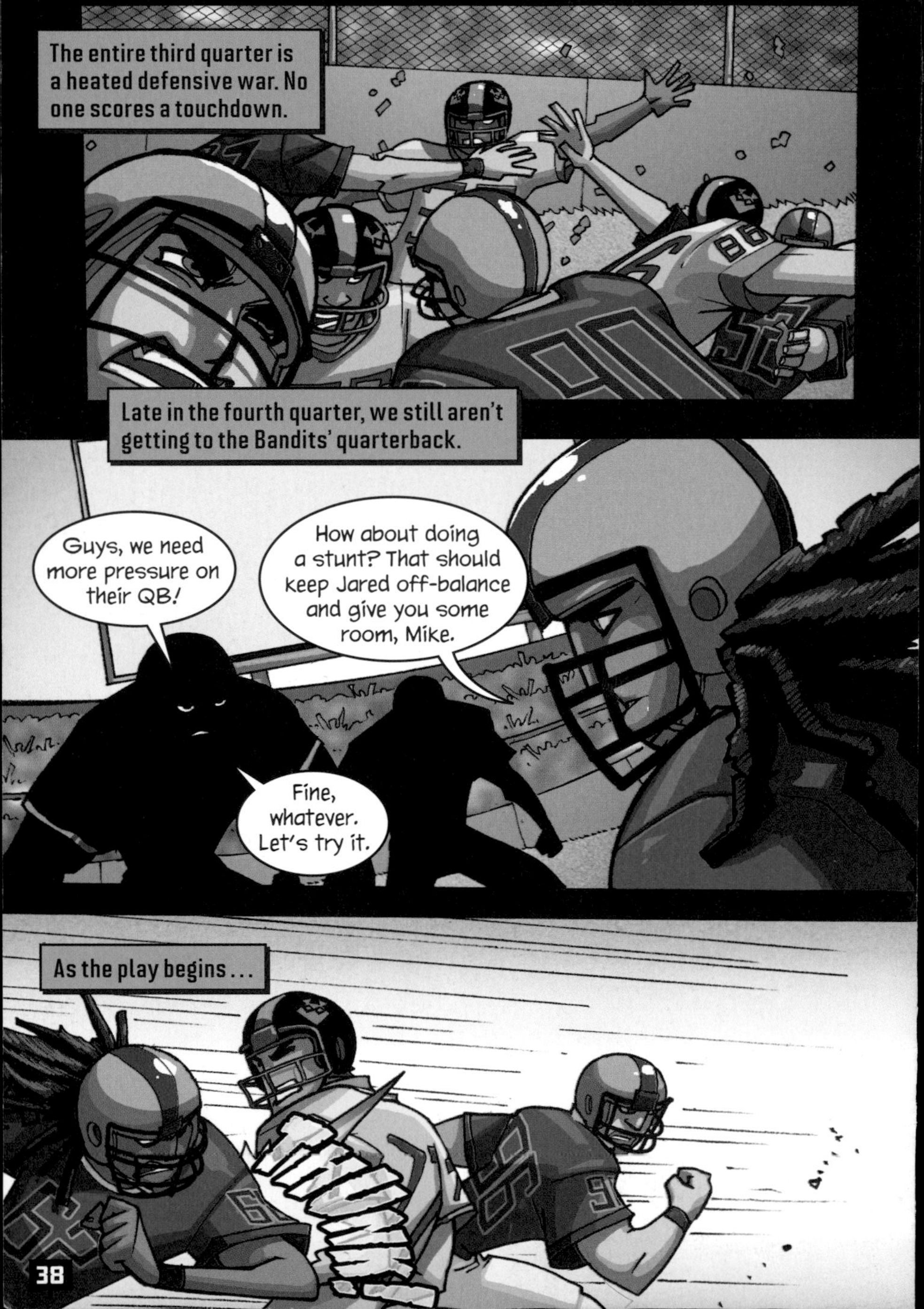

The entire third quarter is a heated defensive war. No one scores a touchdown.
Late in the fourth quarter, we still aren't getting to the Bandits' quarterback.
Guys, we need more pressure on their QB!
How about doing a stunt? That should keep Jared off-balance and give you some room, Mike.
Fine, whatever. Let's try it.
As the play begins . . .

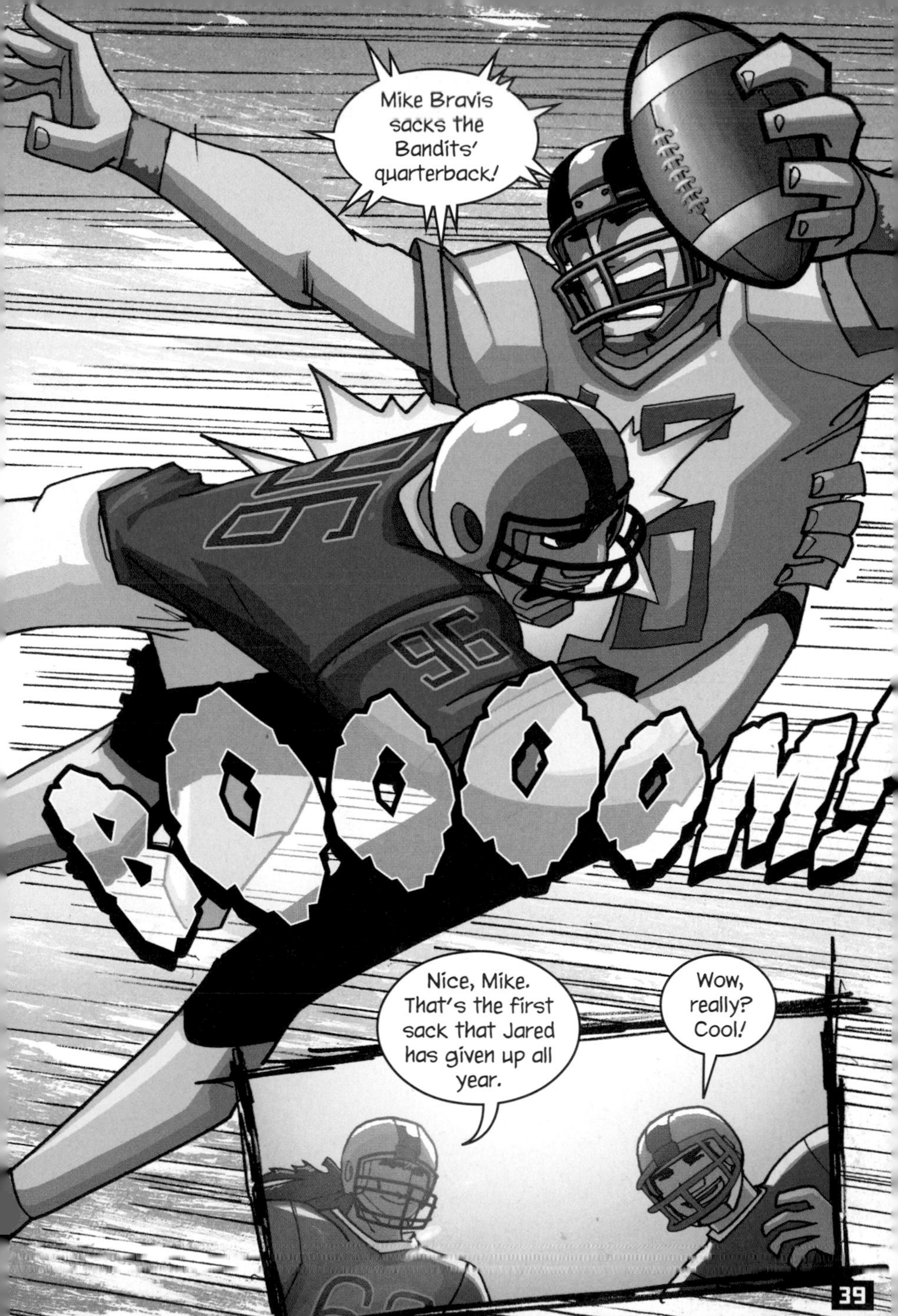

Mike Bravis sacks the Bandits' quarterback!
BOOOOM!
Nice, Mike. That's the first sack that Jared has given up all year.
Wow, really? Cool!

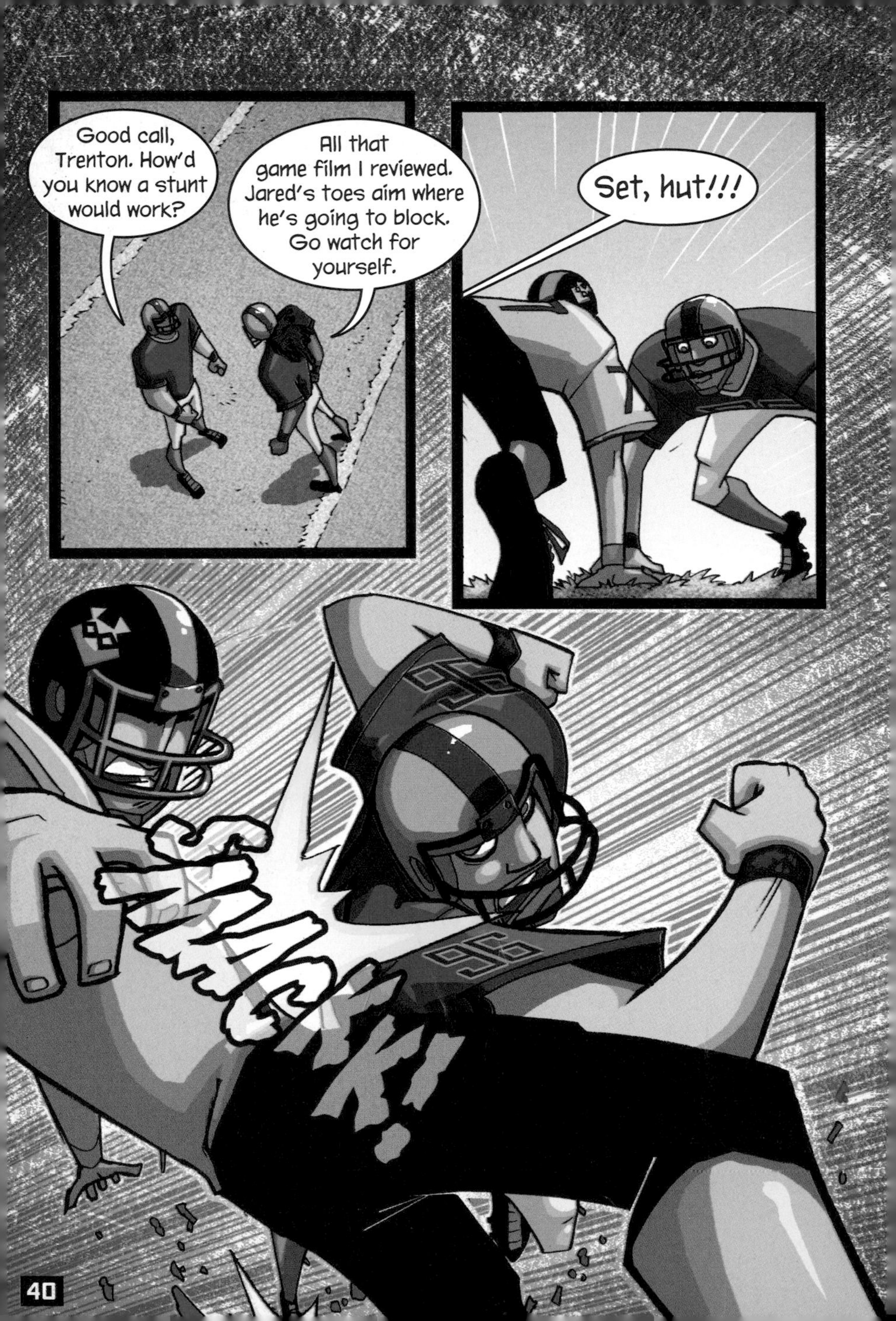

Good call, Trenton. How'd you know a stunt would work?
All that game film I reviewed. Jared's toes aim where he's going to block. Go watch for yourself.
Set, hut!!!

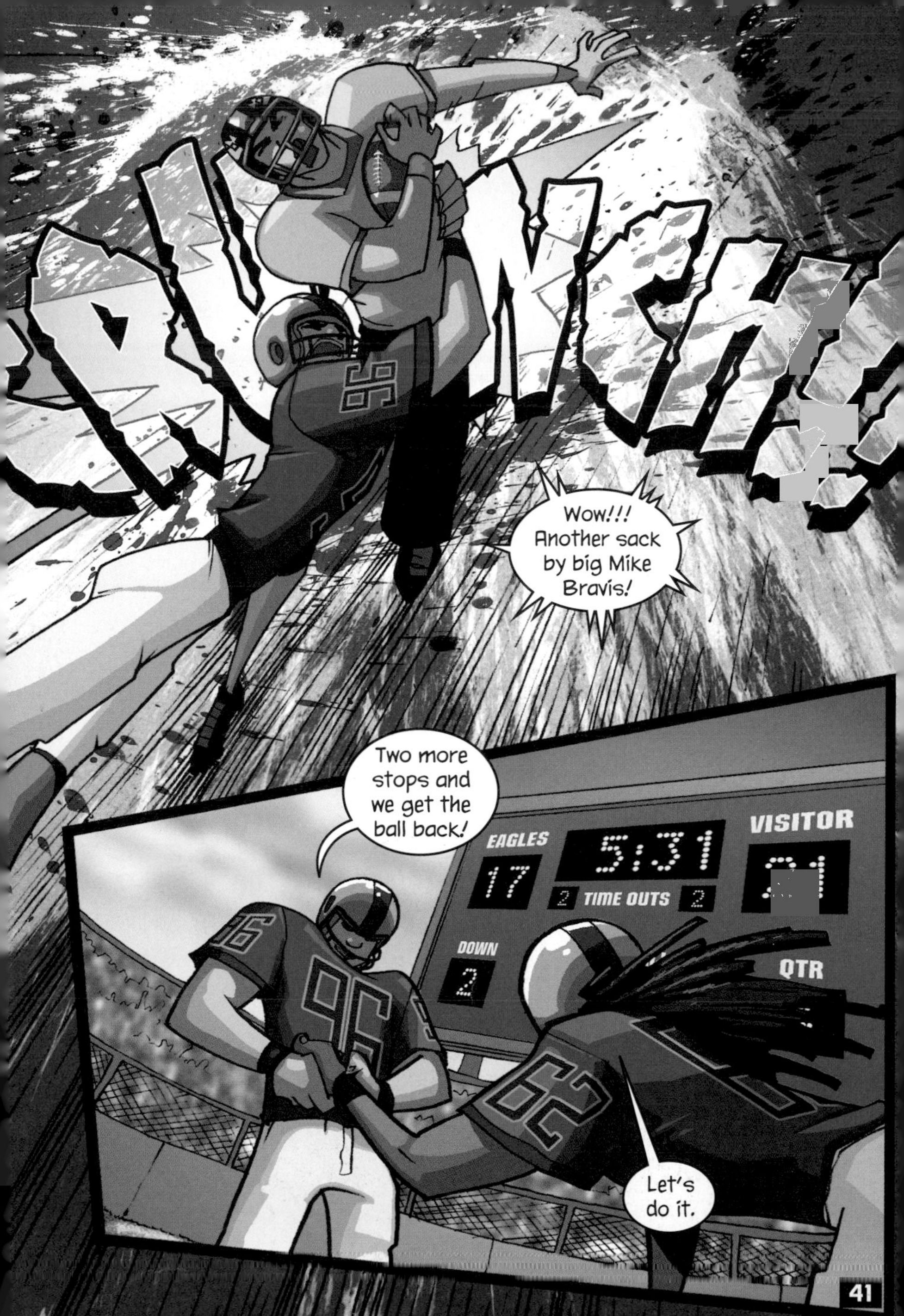
Wow!!! Another sack by big Mike Bravis!
Two more stops and we get the ball back!
EAGLES
17
5:31
VISITOR
2 TIME OUTS 2
DOWN
2
QTR
Let's do it.

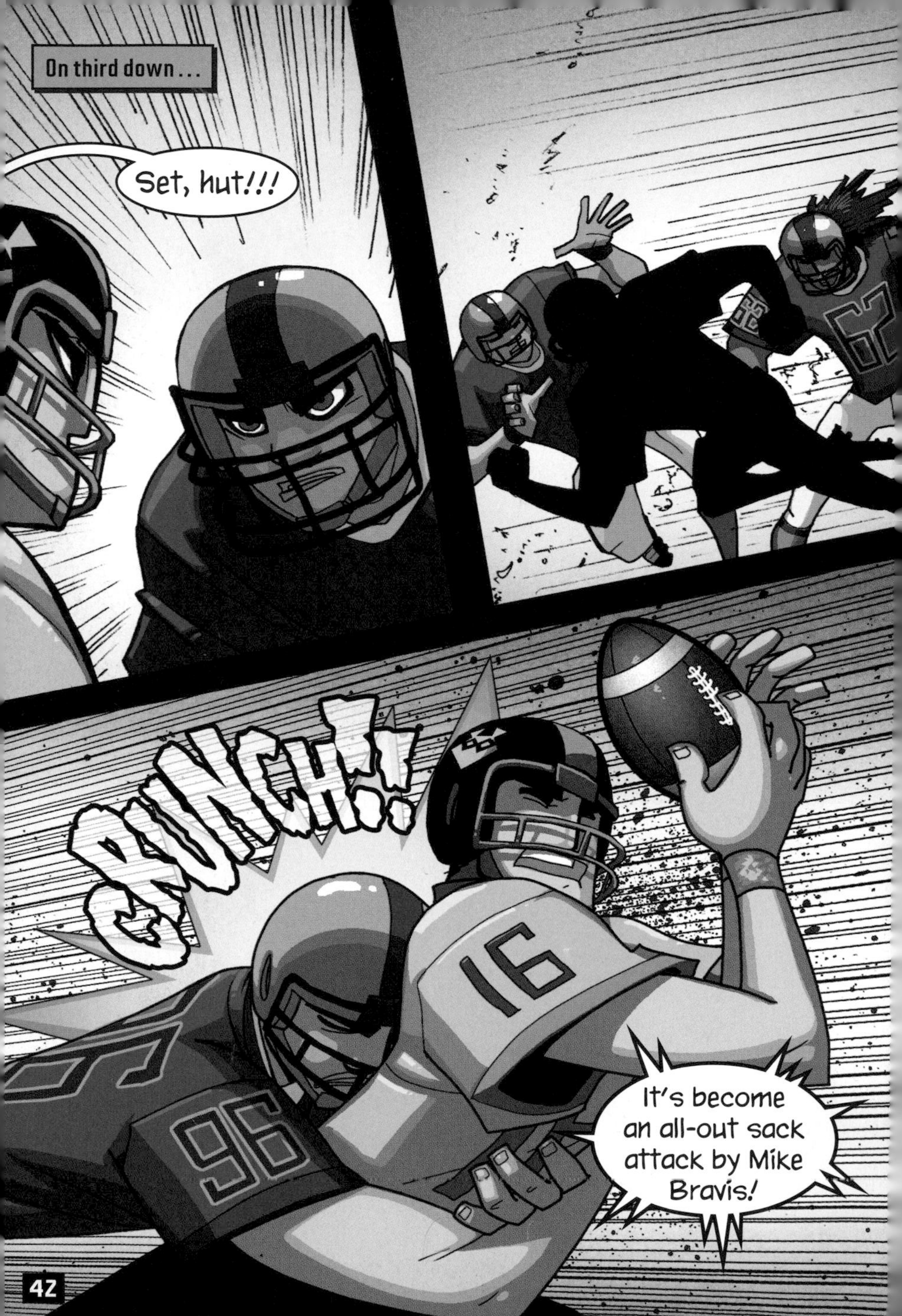
On third down...
Set, hut!!!
CRUNCH!!
It's become an all-out sack attack by Mike Bravis!

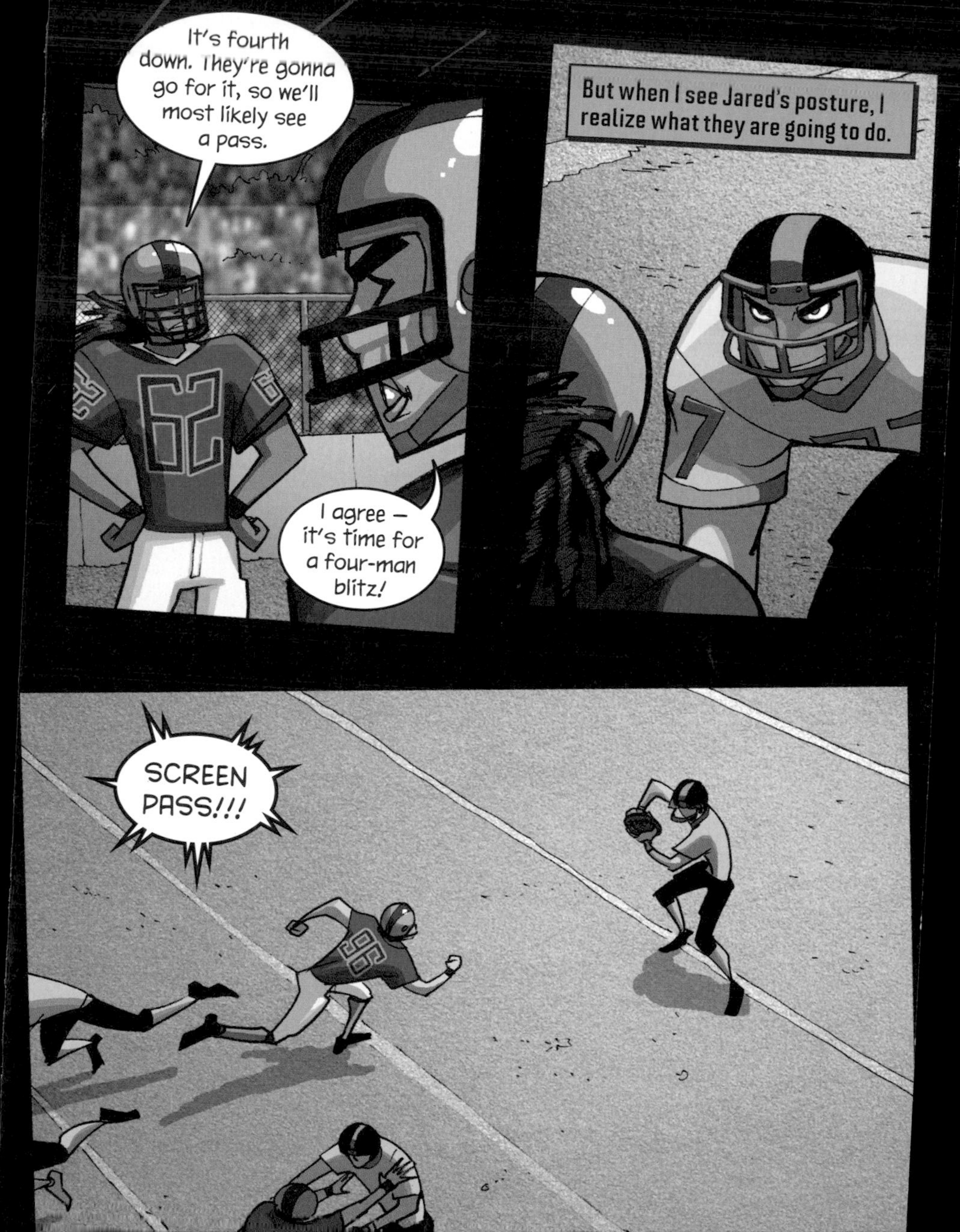
It's fourth down. They're gonna go for it, so we'll most likely see a pass.
I agree — it's time for a four-man blitz!
But when I see Jared's posture, I realize what they are going to do.
SCREEN PASS!!!

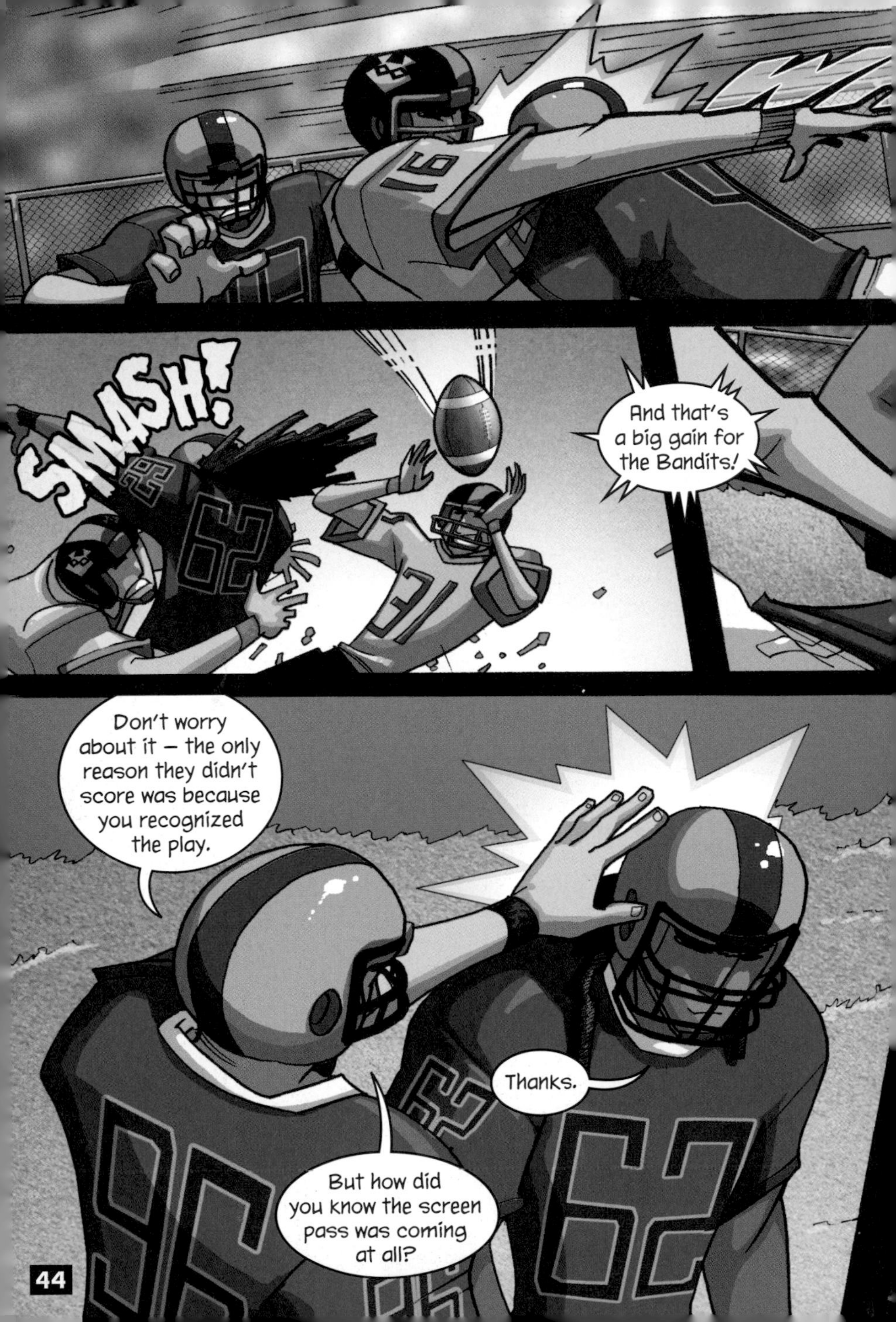
SMASH!
And that's a big gain for the Bandits!
Don't worry about it — the only reason they didn't score was because you recognized the play.
Thanks.
But how did you know the screen pass was coming at all?

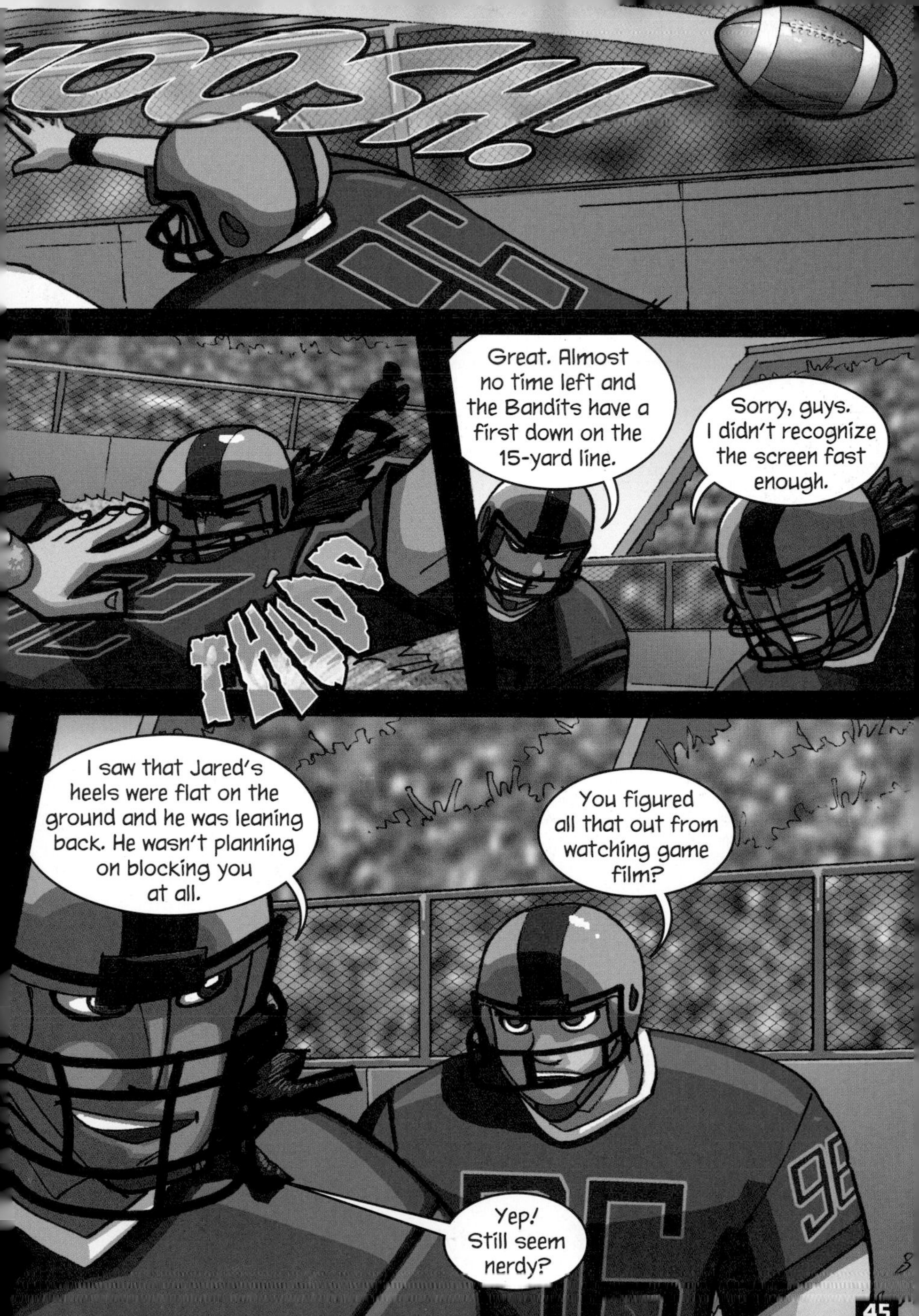
THUD
Great. Almost no time left and the Bandits have a first down on the 15-yard line.
Sorry, guys. I didn't recognize the screen fast enough.
I saw that Jared's heels were flat on the ground and he was leaning back. He wasn't planning on blocking you at all.
You figured all that out from watching game film?
Yep! Still seem nerdy?

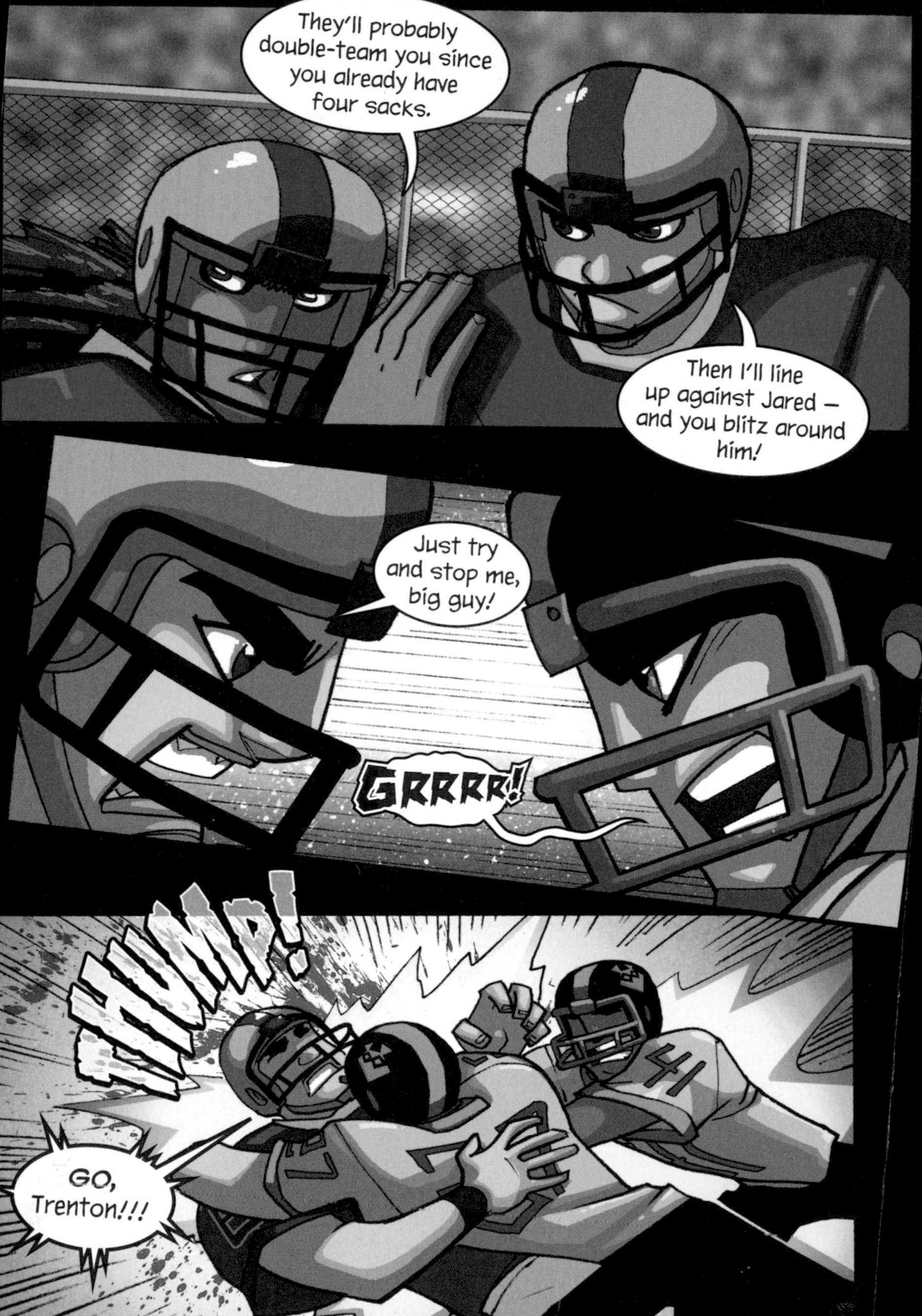
They'll probably double-team you since you already have four sacks.
Then I'll line up against Jared — and you blitz around him!
Just try and stop me, big guy!
GRRRR!
THUMP!
GO, Trenton!!!

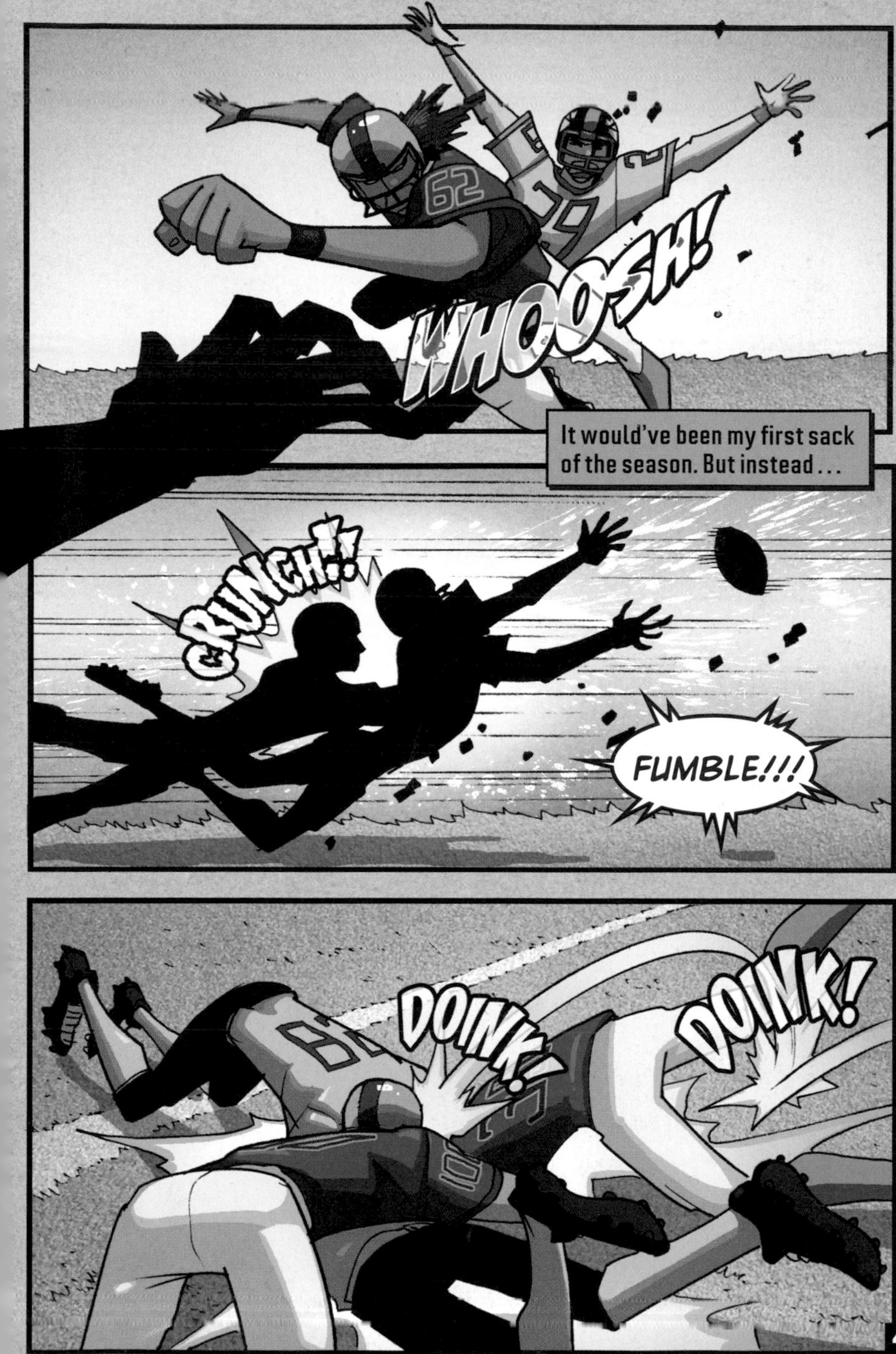
WHOOSH!
It would've been my first sack of the season. But instead . . .
CRUNCH!!
FUMBLE!!!
DOINK!
DOINK!

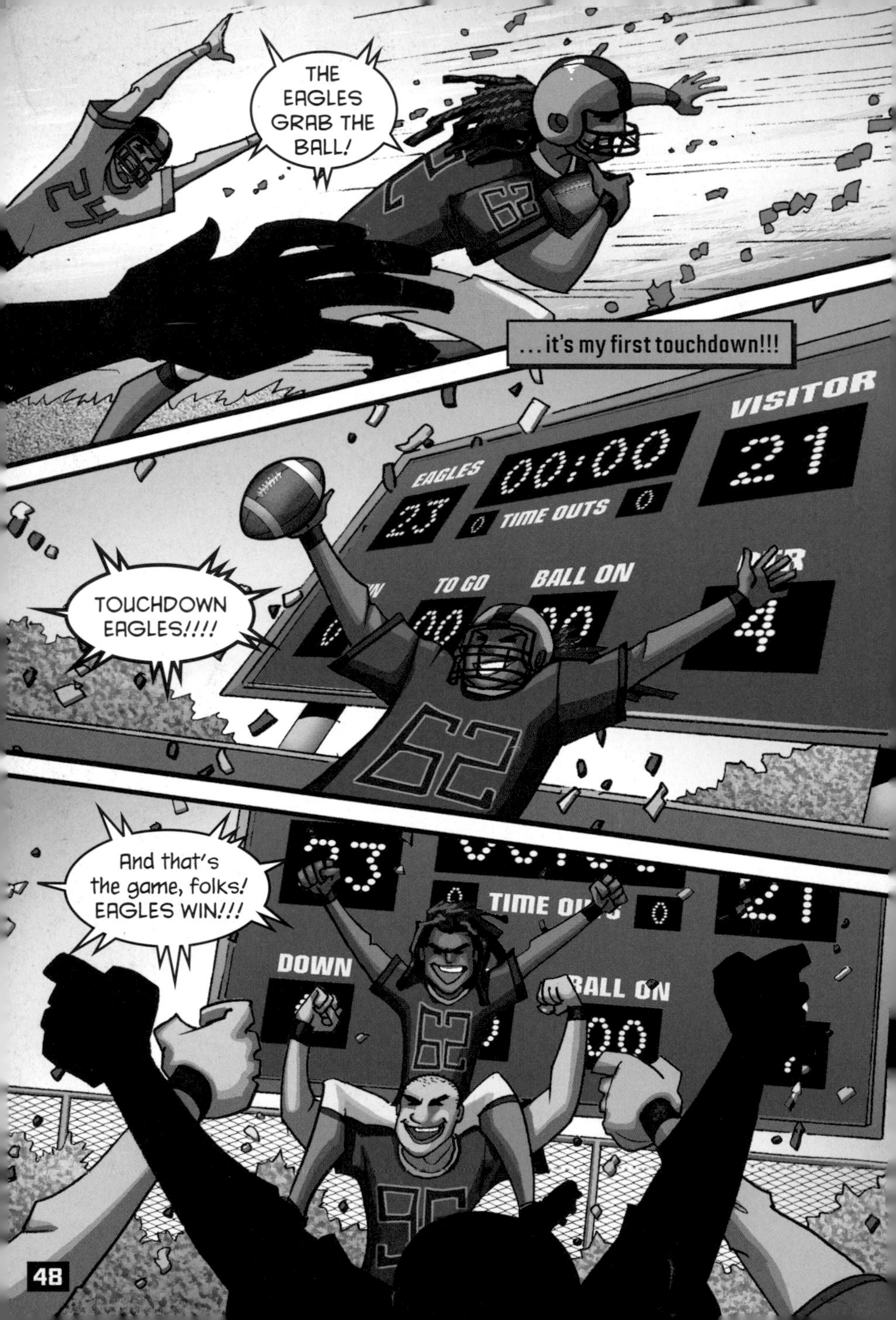
THE EAGLES GRAB THE BALL!
. . . it's my first touchdown!!!
VISITOR
EAGLES
00:00
21
23
TIME OUTS
TO GO
BALL ON
4
TOUCHDOWN EAGLES!!!!
And that's the game, folks! EAGLES WIN!!!
DOWN
BALL ON

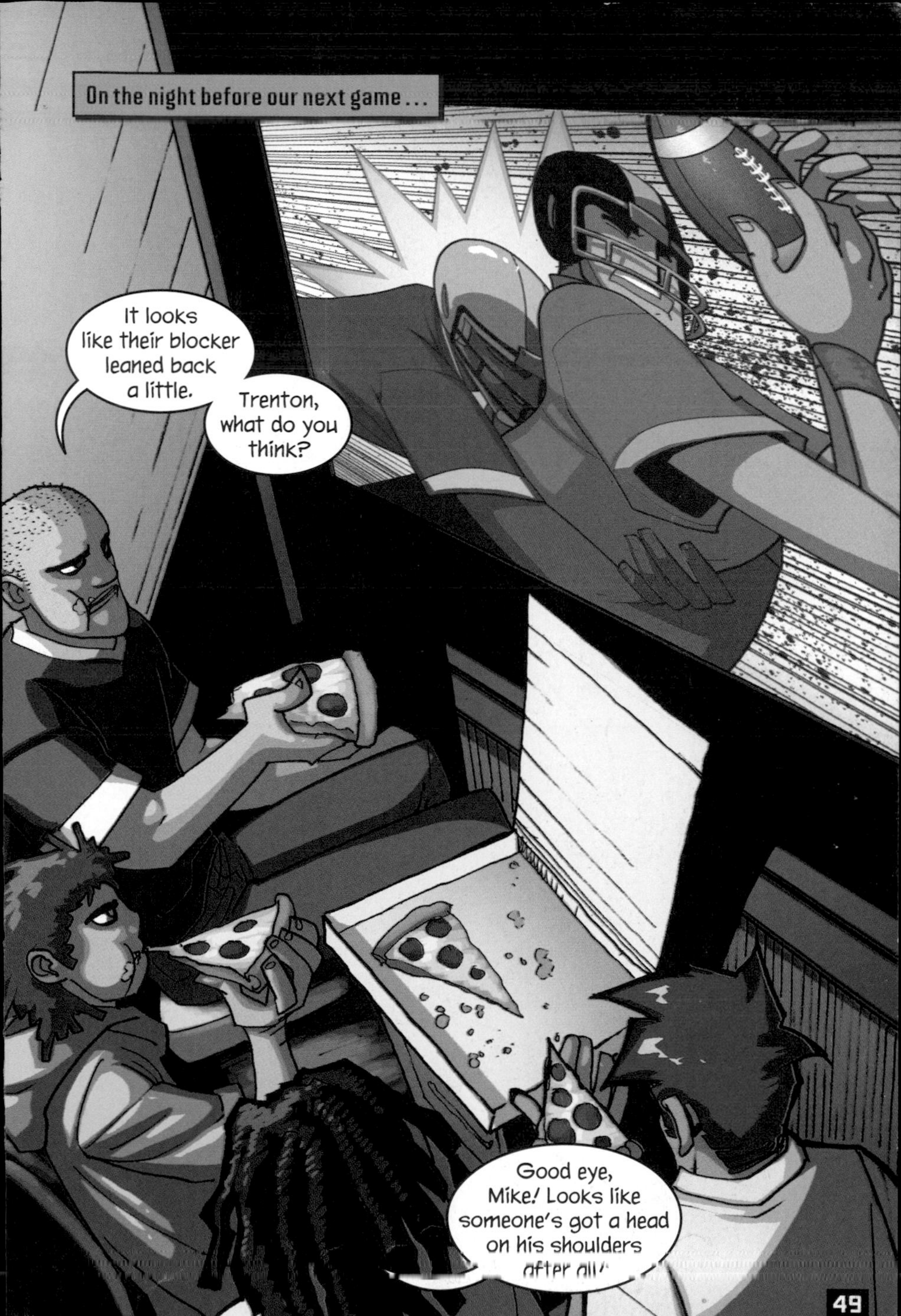
On the night before our next game . . .
It looks like their blocker leaned back a little.
Trenton, what do you think?
Good eye, Mike! Looks like someone's got a head on his shoulders after all!

SPORTS ZONE
POSTGAME RECAP

FBL
FOOTBALL

PNT
PAINTBALL

SOC
SOCCER

BSL
BASEBALL

BBL
BASKETBALL

HKY

EAGLES D-LINE LAUNCHES AN UNSTOPPABLE SACK ATTACK!

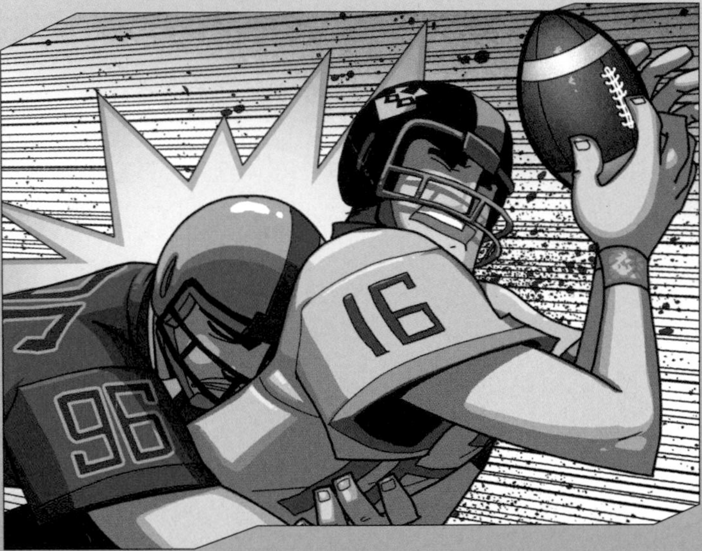

16
96

BY THE NUMBERS

STATS LEADERS:
TACKLES: TRENTON, 11
SACKS: BRAVIS, 5

STORY: Mike Bravis and Trenton Kubrick completely turned things around to help take down the Bandits. At first, both defensive linemen struggled to get to the quarterback. But after a meeting of the minds — and muscles — both boys stepped up their games and took everyone by surprise. Mike explained the situation, saying, "Trenton taught me that muscles are useless without brains to back them up."

Sports Illustrated KIDS

UP NEXT: SI KIDS INFO CENTER

SZ POSTGAME *EXTRA*

WHERE *YOU* ANALYZE THE GAME!

BLZ vs BKS
3:1
TGR vs RDR
33:32
EAG vs BAN
14:7
SPA vs WLD
4:3
BAN vs RDR
21:15
RDR vs LIG
4:3
BLZ vs BKS
3:1

Football fans got a real treat today when the Eagles faced off against the Bandits in a memorable gridiron battle. Let's go into the stands and ask some fans for their opinions on the day's big game...

DISCUSSION QUESTION 1

Mike is strong and fast. Trenton is smart and studious. Which skill set do you think is more important when it comes to playing football? Why?

DISCUSSION QUESTION 2

Mike teases Trenton for studying film instead of going out for pizza with them. Why do you think they made fun of him? Discuss your answers.

WRITING PROMPT 1

At first, Mike and Trenton don't get along because they see some things very differently. Have you ever had an enemy who became a friend? Write about your friends and enemies.

WRITING PROMPT 2

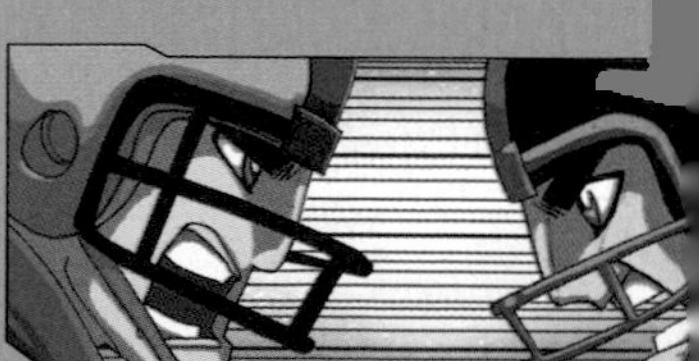

Football is a difficult sport. Which position is the most difficult? What kinds of skills do you need to play that position? Write about it.

Sports Illustrated KIDS

INFO CENTER

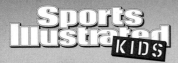

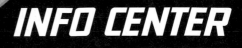

GLOSSARY

BLITZ (BLITS)—a play where one or more defenders rush straight for the quarterback

PASS PROTECTION (PASS pruh-TEK-shuhn)—a blocking scheme players use to keep the defense from getting to the quarterback

RECOGNIZED (REK-uhg-nized)—saw something and knew what it was

SACK (SAK)—a defensive player earns a sack if he tackles the quarterback behind the line of scrimmage

STUNT (STUHNT)—a pass-rushing play where two defensive linemen switch up their routes to the quarterback to try to confuse their blockers

SUPERIOR (soo-PEER-ee-ur)—higher or better

SWEEP (SWEEP)—an offensive play where one or more offensive linemen run toward the outside in order to block for the ball carrier or receiver

CREATORS

Blake A. Hoena › Author

Blake A. Hoena grew up in central Wisconsin, where, in his youth, he wrote stories about robots conquering the Moon and trolls lumbering around in the woods behind his parent's house. Since then, Blake has written more than forty books for children, including *Kickoff Blitz* and *Spotlight Striker*.

Gerardo Sandoval › Illustrator

Gerardo Sandoval is a professional comic book illustrator from Mexico. He has worked on many well-known comics including Tomb Raider books from Top Cow Production. He has also worked on designs for posters and card sets.

Benny Fuentes › Colorist

Benny Fuentes lives in Villahermosa, Tabasco in Mexico, where the temperature is just as hot as the sauce. He studied graphic design in college, but now he works as a full-time colorist in the comic book and graphic novel industry for companies like Marvel, DC Comics, and Top Cow Productions. He shares his home with two crazy cats, Chelo and Kitty, who act like they own the place.

BEN PAULSON IN:

QUARTERBACK SCRAMBLE

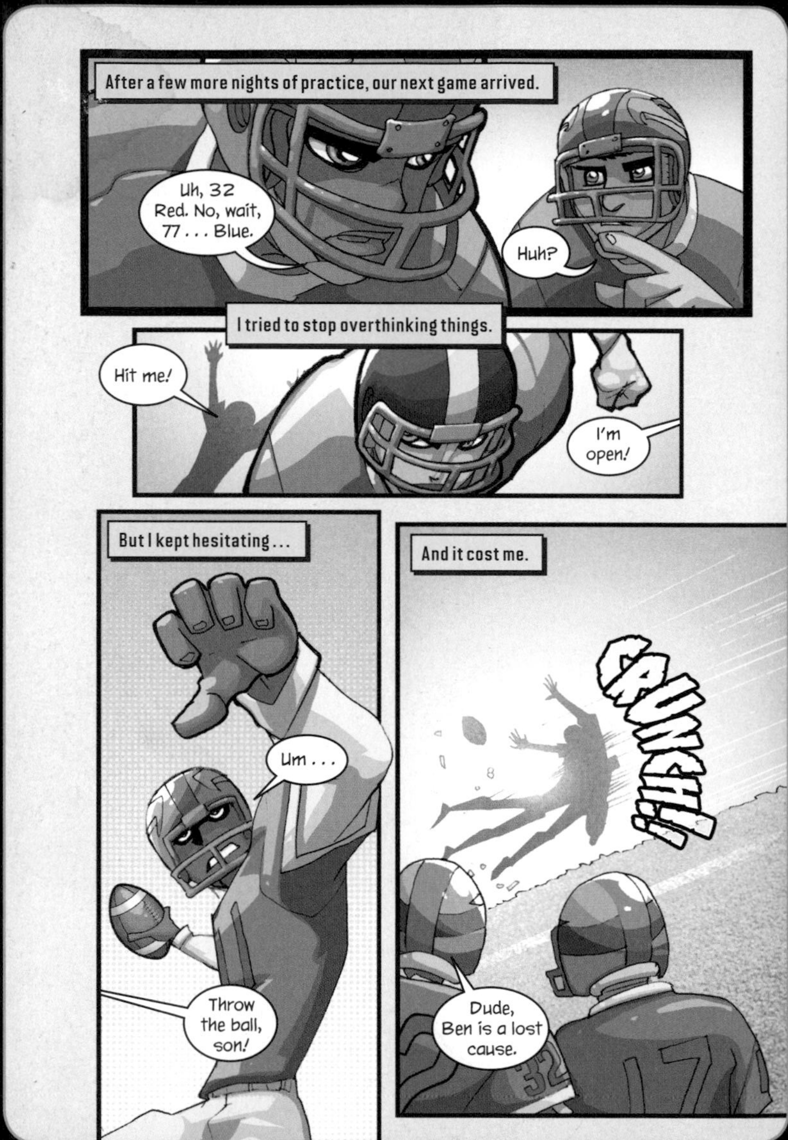
After a few more nights of practice, our next game arrived.
Uh, 32 Red. No, wait, 77 . . . Blue.
Huh?
I tried to stop overthinking things.
Hit me!
I'm open!
But I kept hesitating . . .
Um . . .
Throw the ball, son!
And it cost me.
CRUNCH!!
Dude, Ben is a lost cause.

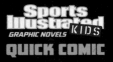

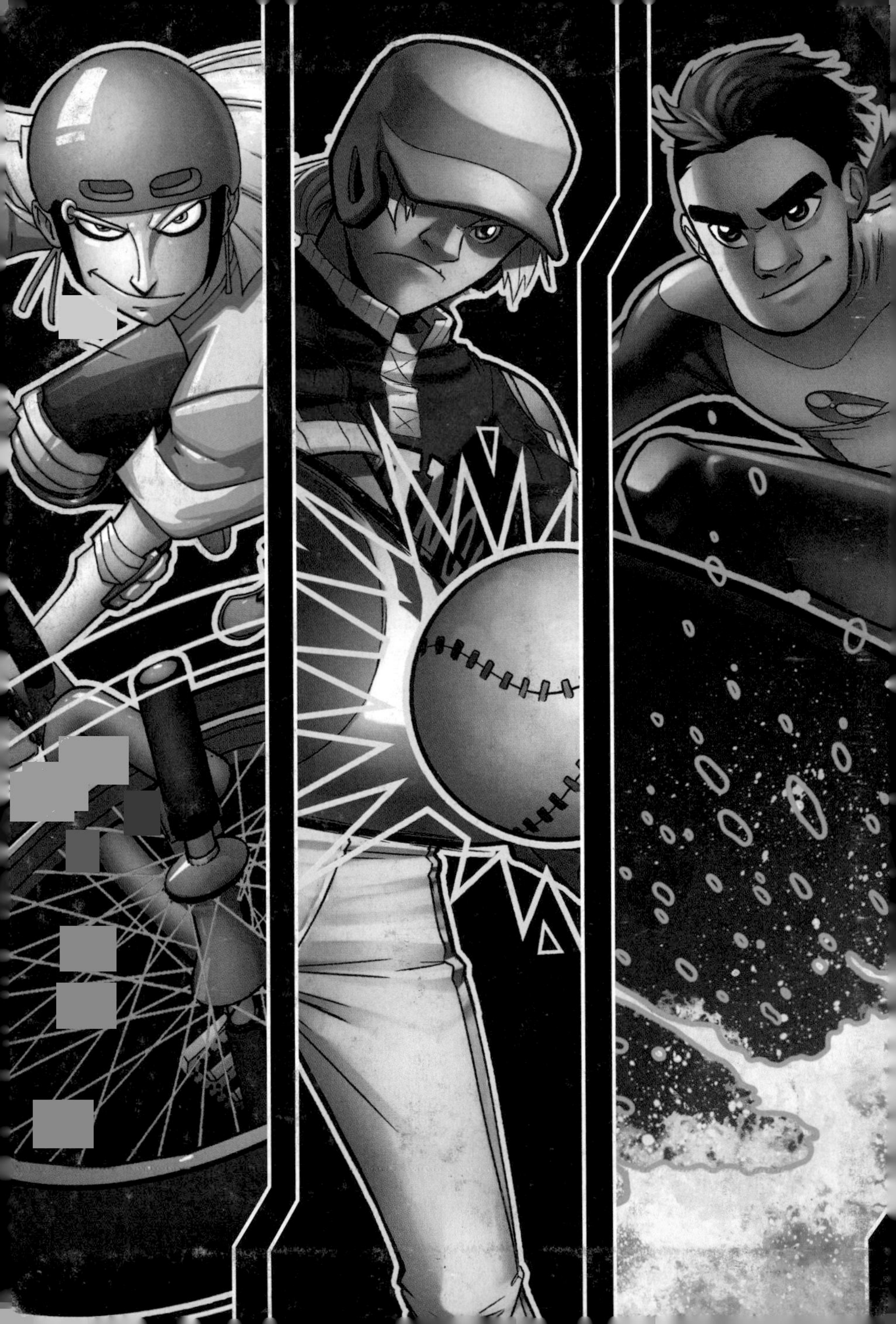